FRANKENSTEIN AND THE PATCHWORK MAN

BBC CHILDREN'S BOOKS

UK | USA | Canada | Ireland | Australia
India | New Zealand | South Africa

BBC Children's Books are published by Puffin Books,
part of the Penguin Random House group of companies
whose addresses can be found at global.penguinrandomhouse.com.

www.penguin.co.uk   www.puffin.co.uk   www.ladybird.co.uk

First published 2025
002

Written by Jack Heath
Copyright © BBC, 2025

BBC, DOCTOR WHO, CYBERMEN and TARDIS (word marks and logos) are trademarks of the
British Broadcasting Corporation and are used under licence. BBC logo © BBC 1996.
DOCTOR WHO logo and WHO insignia © BBC 2018. Dalek image © BBC/Terry Nation 1963.

The moral right of the author and copyright holders has been asserted

No part of this book may be used or reproduced in any manner for the
purpose of training artificial intelligence technologies or systems. In accordance
with Article 4(3) of the DSM Directive 2019/790, Penguin Random
House expressly reserves this work from the text and data mining exception.

Set in 11.5/15.5pt Bembo Book MT Std
Typeset by Jouve (UK), Milton Keynes
Printed and bound in Great Britain by Clays Ltd, Elcograf S.p.A.

The authorized representative in the EEA is Penguin Random House Ireland,
Morrison Chambers, 32 Nassau Street, Dublin D02 YH68

A CIP catalogue record for this book is available from the British Library

ISBN: 978-1-405-96526-2

All correspondence to:
BBC Children's Books, Penguin Random House Children's UK
One Embassy Gardens, 8 Viaduct Gardens London SW11 7BW

Penguin Random House is committed to a
sustainable future for our business, our readers
and our planet. This book is made from Forest
Stewardship Council® certified paper.

Frankenstein and the Patchwork Man

JACK HEATH

PUFFIN

For Ian and Barbara, my first companions

Prologue

*B*eware.

The Patchwork Man froze. The thought had not been his own – it had a fizzing, buzzing quality, like a swarm of bees in his brain stem.

They were talking to him. He had learned not to ignore *Them*.

He slipped behind the thick trunk of an oak tree and turned his big head, mismatched vertebrae clicking as he scanned the clearing. The canopy was still and silent in the afternoon light. The birds had flown away when they saw him coming, the squirrels disappearing into their holes, hedgehogs cowering in their burrows. Even the insects had vanished. It was as if no living thing could bear to look upon him.

Beware, They said again. The buzzing grew louder, a tingle running down his spine, making his toes twitch inside his leather boots.

Soon, he saw it. A loop of wire, half-buried in the leaf litter ahead. He moved closer, his misshapen limbs creaking with each heavy step. A stone slab came into view, balanced on a bough high above, bound in thick rope. If he stepped in the loop, he would presumably be pulled into the air by his ankle while the counterweight descended. Then he would be trapped here until the Doctor came for him. Unpicked his stitches. Pulled him apart.

The Patchwork Man bent over, touched his fingertips to the ground and closed his eyes. The energy surged down his arm and vibrated the dirt, breaking up the clods and making it as soft as sand. He pushed his hand into the ground and found something solid – a tree root. He crushed it in his giant fist and wrenched the broken wood upward, soil cascading off the sides. Then he made his way back over to the trap.

He was about to toss the severed limb into the wire loop, triggering the counterweight, when he heard something: a wheezing, groaning sound, like a set of bellows.

He whirled round in time to see something take shape in the fog – a tall blue box with a flashing light on top. He stared at it, his hand still clenched round the broken root. Was this another of the Doctor's tricks?

Whatever it was, it wouldn't stand between him and his revenge.

The Patchwork Man tossed the tree root into the thick shrubbery, leaving the trap untouched. Then he walked away from the blue box, melting into the mist and shadow.

The Haunted Forest

Rose Tyler followed the Doctor out of the TARDIS and looked around. They were in a dense, silent forest. The trees were gnarled and twisted, the leaves withered or long since fallen. The dirt was damp underfoot, and a cold fog drenched everything.

She turned round and tried to re-enter the TARDIS.

'Oh, no you don't.' The Doctor grabbed her shoulder and steered her away from the door. 'This will be the experience of a lifetime, and I won't let you miss it.'

Easy for him to say. His leather coat was warmer than her denim jacket, and he was six feet tall – his big ears were slightly *above* the fog. Rose was only five foot five, just short enough to be swallowed up by it. Even on tiptoes, she could hardly see.

And she was getting nervous about the Doctor's plan. 'I'm not sure I want to get surgery from an alien,' she said. 'Or anyone, actually.'

'You'll love it! Having four arms is twice as good as having two. That's just maths.' Beaming, the Doctor locked the door of the TARDIS with a little silver key. 'There are some cultures where basic sign language requires at least three hands, and trust me, you *really* don't want to be misunderstood by a Quellorian Warrior.'

Rose raised an eyebrow. 'Are we expecting to meet any of those?'

'Nothing's impossible,' the Doctor said.

Rose looked doubtfully at the gloomy forest. She liked adventures, but would it kill the Doctor to take her to a day spa once in a while? Rose quite liked those massage chairs in shopping centres. Imagine how good they might be a hundred years into the future.

'Either way,' she said, 'I don't think Mickey would be too impressed if I came home with extra limbs.'

Disappointment flickered over the Doctor's face, perhaps because Rose had reminded him that she had a life back on Earth, and that their adventures would someday end. But his irrepressible grin soon returned.

'You might be surprised,' he replied cheerfully. 'It doesn't matter though, because they'll remove the add-ons before you leave. Proprietary technology, you see. They were *very* unimpressed when I tried to walk away with a third heart.'

'Remove?' Rose repeated. 'If there's one thing I like less than the idea of having arms added, it's having them *chopped off*.' Again, she tried to return to the TARDIS, but the Doctor blocked her path.

'Don't be like that,' he said. 'Have I ever put you in harm's way?'

She crossed her arms over her chest. 'Many, many times.'

'All right, but have I ever not gotten you out of it again?'

'If I lose an arm, my mum will be furious. With *you*. And you don't want to get on Mum's bad side.'

'You're telling me. I can still feel that slap.' The Doctor touched his face. 'Don't worry, the surgeons always ask which limbs are the originals before they fire up the ... hmm.' He looked around as though he'd finally noticed the forest they were standing in. 'That's odd.'

'What is?' Rose asked uneasily. Usually, they'd wander around for a bit before the Doctor said, 'That's odd.' This time, they hadn't even made it three steps away from the TARDIS.

'The transhumanists of Tyronica Prime aren't big on trees.' The Doctor waded through the slush of rotting leaves and mud. Rose followed, tucking her hands into her armpits to keep them warm.

'Everyone likes trees,' she said.

'Not them. Hydroponic oxygen gardens, yes, but not whatever species this is.' He produced his sonic screwdriver and waved it around like a wizard casting a spell. It buzzed, bathing the tree in an eerie blue glow.

Rose had never quite figured out the limits of the sonic's capabilities. She knew it could sometimes bounce sound waves off objects to determine what they were made of, or make things vibrate at various frequencies to either fix or break them. But she wasn't sure what it could do to an ordinary tree.

'That's just an oak tree,' she said.

'I think you'll find it's *actually* –' the Doctor briefly studied his sonic, though it didn't have a screen – 'an oak tree, yes. Why would oak trees be growing on Tyronica Prime?'

Rose sighed. 'Maybe because we're not on Tyronica Prime. I bet we're within ten miles of Cardiff. Again.'

TARDIS stood for Time And Relative Dimension In Space. It was a stolen – 'borrowed', the Doctor would say – vehicle, capable of transporting them to any point in the fabric of space-time. Anywhere, anywhen. This made it all the more frustrating when it took them to the wrong spot. The Doctor claimed to know how to pilot the ship, but Rose wasn't convinced. The TARDIS could also, in theory, camouflage itself to match its surroundings. In practice, it always resembled a blue police box, so it looked out of place everywhere except 1960s London.

'Hmm.' The Doctor bounced on his toes, perhaps testing the planet's gravity. He sniffed the air with his impressive nose. 'Hardly any nitrogen oxide in the atmosphere – wherever we are, they haven't invented the diesel engine yet. If this *is* Earth, it's the eighteen hundreds at the latest.'

'And yet . . .' Rose pointed to a smoother, straighter trunk nearby.

The Doctor frowned. 'Ooh. That's not oak.'

'No . . . it's a power pole.'

The Time Lord peered upward, an expression of wonder on his face as he took in the transformer, the cables and the seemingly ordinary brass plaque. Rose tried to stay exasperated, but a smile forced its way through. This was one of her favourite things about the Doctor, the way he was always so delighted to be proven wrong.

'Well, *that's* not right.' The Doctor's sonic screwdriver whirred again. 'Who could be using alternating current at this scale in the eighteen hundreds?'

Rose looked longingly back at the TARDIS. She thought about day spas and massage chairs. Then she thought about how disappointed the Doctor would be if they left without investigating The Mystery of the Very Old Power Pole.

Maybe, by the time they'd solved this puzzle and returned to the TARDIS, he'd have forgotten about collecting extra arms from Tyronica Prime.

She sighed. 'Should we find out?'

The Doctor beamed. 'Rose Tyler, I thought you'd never ask. Come on!' He set off into the woods.

Rose was about to follow, when she felt a tingling at the nape of her neck. She pushed her blonde hair aside and brushed frantically at her skin to find the source of the sensation, just in case there was a spider. But nothing was there. It seemed to be the fog itself, crackling faintly like it had a static charge. And she thought she could hear a low *hum*.

Rose turned in time to see a large bush rustle and go still.

She stared. 'Is someone there?'

The fog swallowed the words and gave nothing back.

Rose took a cautious step towards the bush. The humming grew louder. As she reached for one of the branches, the bush twitched, more violently this time.

Rose jumped back. 'Doctor!'

He didn't reply. Maybe he was already out of earshot. Rose sidestepped so she could see who was behind the bush without getting close to it again . . .

But there was no one. Just dead leaves and mud. Rose was alone in the clearing.

Had she imagined the movement? Or could it have been the wind?

No. During her travels with the Doctor, she'd learned to trust herself. Someone or something had been here. She could still feel its malevolent gaze.

'Rose.'

She whirled round. But it was just the Doctor, who had come back for her.

'You fell behind,' he said. 'Is everything all right?'

'I . . .' Rose hesitated. If the Doctor got side-tracked by The Mystery of the Twitching Shrubbery, they'd be stuck here forever. '. . . just got distracted,' she finished. 'Let's get a move on.'

The Doctor gave her a quizzical look but turned back to the trail. This time, she followed him.

Neither of them saw the giant figure unfold itself from the shadows behind them.

The Charging Ram

What Rose had taken for dawn must have been dusk. The twilight faded as they pushed through the thickening fog, following the power lines overhead. The trees grew more stunted as they walked, twigs rattling in the wind and clawing at Rose's clothes.

'These trees don't look all that healthy,' she observed.

'You're right.' The Doctor approached one of them. 'Are you a conscious entity?' he asked it.

The tree, of course, said nothing.

'Oh, is that so?' the Doctor said, as though it had spoken. 'How awful for you.'

'Are you having a laugh?' Rose demanded.

The Doctor plucked a leaf from one of the branches, sniffed it, and then rubbed it between his fingers. 'Salt,' he said thoughtfully. 'The tree is absorbing it through the roots, then trying to expel it through the leaves.'

'Does that mean there's some kind of salt alien living underground or something?'

'No,' the Doctor said. 'Just means there's too much salt in the groundwater.' He smiled at Rose. 'You humans are so obsessed with aliens! You ignore the miracles right under your noses.'

Rose rolled her eyes. She wasn't sure 'salty water' counted as a miracle, and she was too cold to humour the Doctor. What would happen if they didn't find shelter? The Doctor was full of surprises, but she doubted he had a tent stuffed in any of his pockets.

Soon, they reached the crest of a hill, which gave them a clear view of the mist-soaked landscape. Since boarding the TARDIS, Rose had seen green skies, twin suns, triplet moons and oceans of shimmering mercury. The dark forest below was a little underwhelming.

'We could ask for directions.' Rose pointed towards a wisp of smoke, which betrayed the presence of a chimney less than a kilometre away. Maybe someone there would offer her a cup of tea. She'd kill for a cup of tea.

The Doctor's face broke into a smile. 'Fantastic! Come on.' He jogged down the slope, Rose struggling to keep up with his long stride.

Soon, they reached a dirt road criss-crossed with thin tracks from cart wheels. A crooked wooden sign was sinking into the mud nearby. Rose jogged up to it and squinted in the dim light. The TARDIS had put a psychic field in her head that translated almost any language, written or spoken – but it couldn't compensate for darkness and terrible handwriting.

Rose illuminated the sign with the faint glow from her phone screen. As soon as she could make out the words, she turned to the Doctor, trying not to look smug. 'Would you look at that?' she said. 'Cardiff. Seven miles.'

'All right, all right.' The Doctor put his hands on his hips. 'Why would the TARDIS bring us here?'

'Perhaps you took a wrong turn?'

'Oi! I passed my driving test like everyone else. Took me a few goes, mind. Parallel parking is tricky in four dimensions. But my sense of direction is perfect. We were on our way to Tyronica Prime, and the TARDIS decided to make a stop along the way.'

'We were just on a space station orbiting Mars in the year 2200,' Rose said, 'and then we were trying to get to the Triangulum Galaxy in the year 3000. How could nineteenth-century Cardiff possibly be "on our way"?'

'Firstly, space-time isn't linear. It's more like spaghetti, with strands all tangled up and stuck together. Secondly, we're not in Cardiff. We're much closer to . . .' He trailed off, peering at the sign. '. . . Lamond.' His smile faded, his gaze hardening.

Rose felt that tingling on the back of her neck again. She brushed away the phantom spider, which still didn't exist. 'What's wrong?' she asked.

'I'm not sure.' The Doctor turned in a slow circle. He was looking at the forest, but Rose didn't think he was seeing it. 'Lamond,' he said again. 'Why does that sound so familiar?'

Rose frowned. Actually, it sounded familiar to her, too. 'Isn't that a really salty lake?' she asked. 'My friend Shareen went once, on a summer holiday. She said it was great for swimming, because the salt water makes you float.'

'Well, that would explain why the trees are unwell. Too much salt in the groundwater . . .' The Doctor chewed his lip. 'Hang on, there's a local legend, I'm sure of it. The people of Lamond have this story, like a folk tale. About some kind of creature with mismatched parts. Maybe a lion with the head of a man, who asks riddles . . .?'

'You're thinking of the Sphinx,' Rose said. 'Which I think is Egyptian, not Welsh.'

'Oh. Maybe it was the star man with the mismatched eyes?'

'That's David Bowie, and he's a real person. Or he will be, in like, a hundred years. Mum has an autographed record.'

The Doctor's frown deepened. 'David? He told me his name was Ziggy.'

Rose threw up her hands. 'Is this going to be one of those things you don't remember until much too late? Like, you won't remember it's the village of the giant scorpions until we've already been swallowed by a giant scorpion?'

The Doctor huffed. 'That only happened once.'

'Once was enough,' Rose said. 'Tell me, what's the point of experiencing everything in the universe if you can't remember any of it?'

'I haven't experienced *everything*. I've visited less than one per cent of inhabited planets in less than *point* one per cent of centuries. Secondly, the more things you've done, the harder it is to remember them all. Why do you think old people get confused?'

'I assumed it was a side-effect from powdered custard, or something.'

'Well, that stuff can be dangerous,' the Doctor admitted. 'A factory caught fire in 1981, Oxfordshire. The smell was delicious.' The Doctor caught Rose's look and rolled his eyes. 'Don't worry. No one was killed.'

Rose relaxed. 'Phew.'

'Just very, very badly burned,' the Doctor went on, ignoring Rose's horrified stare. 'Anyway, let's ask the locals if custard creams have been invented yet.' He checked the sign a final time, nodded to himself, then marched ahead, humming 'Life on Mars'. Rose followed, keeping an eye out for scorpions.

Soon, they reached the kind of village Rose might have called 'charming' if she didn't want to offend anyone by mentioning the odour. The buildings were a mixture of stone hovels and wooden huts with thatched roofs. The main street had probably once been dirt, but now it was equal parts mud and horse manure. Bitter smoke wisped upward from crooked chimneys. A brown pig with a white nose shuffled past, belly wobbling. There was no other movement, and the quiet was oppressive. Rose couldn't see anybody in the darkness behind the empty window-frames, but nevertheless, she felt watched.

'Where is everybody?' she whispered.

'Not used to strangers, I suppose,' the Doctor murmured back. 'Don't worry. We'll win them over.'

Rose wrinkled her nose as they passed a rusted water trough, fetid mushrooms growing round the edges. 'Can't wait.'

They walked on in silence through the deserted narrow streets until the road opened up into a modest town square. A large stone well stood at its centre and, beside it, a wooden post with two pieces of parchment nailed to the front. The ink looked like it had run before it dried, so the messages were written in a font Rose would have described as 'horror movie sans'.

The Doctor peered at one of the notices. 'There's a curfew in effect. No one is allowed out after sunset, and no one is allowed in the forest at any time, by order of . . . someone. Can't make out the signature.'

Rose looked around. The sun was setting. Maybe everyone had already gone into their hovels. One of the things she'd noticed when visiting the past was how early people went to bed prior to the invention of electric lighting.

The pig had climbed on to the wall. It stared solemnly at her.

'Hello,' Rose said, waving awkwardly.

The pig's hairy white nose twitched.

'Where is everybody?' she asked.

She didn't really expect a response. But the pig growled at her like a wary bulldog.

Rose backed away. 'Doctor?'

The Doctor whirled round, whipped out his sonic screwdriver and buzzed it at the pig. He glanced at the device and then put it back in his pocket. 'Just a pig,' he said cheerfully, and turned back to the parchment.

Rose did not feel reassured. She was a city girl, unused to farm animals, and for all she knew, normal pigs could be vicious. She'd seen a Guy Ritchie movie on the telly where a gangster used pigs to dispose of his victims. But just as she was looking around for a stick, a rock or some other kind of weapon, the pig sniffed the air, then leapt off its perch and scampered away into the darkness.

Rose sighed with relief and turned to the Doctor, who was studying the second piece of parchment.

'What do you make of this?' he asked.

Rose pinched the corner of the notice to stop it from flapping in the breeze. There was a primitive sketch of a big man in a big coat, wearing a pilgrim's hat. His face was hidden in shadow, all except for a broad chin with a scar across it. He looked like one of the waxworks from the medieval torture bit of Madame Tussauds. Underneath the sketch were the words, IF SEEN RING BELL.

She looked around to see that there was indeed a bell, about the size of a football, crudely bolted to a pole beside the well.

'So is this person wanted by the police, or something?' she asked.

The Doctor let go of the notice and put his hands on his hips. 'No crimes listed. No reward. Just a warning, by the looks of it. Steer clear of this guy, that sort of thing.'

'I suppose.' Rose didn't think she would need to be warned to avoid a man who looked like that.

At the end of the street stood a tavern, its wooden sign creaking in the breeze. A name was carved into it in surprisingly delicate lettering: *The Charging Ram*. A flickering glow emanated from within and Rose could hear hushed, anxious voices. Nothing like the songs and laughter she'd hear from outside the Spinning Wheel, or any London pub for that matter.

'Fancy a pint?' the Doctor asked her.

'Here?!'

'All right, how about a lemon, lime and bitters?'

Rose couldn't suppress a snort. No matter how dire things looked, the Doctor could always make her laugh.

'All right, go on, then,' she said.

The tavern was a hodgepodge of stone and timber, the entrance marked not by a door but by a pair of oily curtains, which nevertheless kept the evening chill out. As Rose stepped into the gloomy interior, the voices abruptly ceased, leaving only the quiet burble of a simmering cauldron perched precariously on an open fire pit at one end of the room. The aroma hinted at turnips and leeks.

A dozen or so townspeople occupied wooden stools and benches scattered around rough-hewn tables. They were clad in worn riding gear or soiled work aprons – the kind that suggested long days tending fields or mending fences. Their conversations halted mid-sentence as heads turned in unison towards Rose and the Doctor. Rose felt a sea of suspicious eyes on her.

'Hello!' The Doctor gave a cheerful wave. 'I'm the Doctor; this is Rose.'

The townspeople said nothing. The fire crackled softly under the cauldron.

Unconcerned, the Doctor made his way over to the bar. As she followed, Rose noticed a young woman who seemed out of place. Her long, dark hair was pinned up elaborately, her cheeks dusted with rouge and her dress made of fine fabric with delicate stitching. She sat as though posing for a portrait. The tavern was crowded, but the seats around her were empty, except for one. A slight blonde girl in a plain smock sat beside her, like the world's least intimidating bodyguard.

Rose gave the posh woman a little smile. The woman didn't return it. She grimaced and turned her head back towards the window, as if she could tell Rose was just a shop assistant who lived with her mum in a South London flat.

Fine, Rose thought. She went to the bar and perched on a crooked stool beside the Doctor. Slowly, hushed chatter filled the room again.

In contrast to the simple furnishings around the room, the bar was a masterpiece of craftsmanship. The mahogany surface was inlaid with intricate carvings, tiny reliefs of snakes and men and women. Rose gently ran her fingers over the design, tracing the grooves.

'It's an apple tree,' said a voice from behind her.

She turned to see a burly, red-bearded man with small eyes in wrinkled sockets. His canvas shirt hung open, and his thick arms were crossed over a broad, hairy chest.

'Carved it myself,' he added.

Rose could see it now – all the tiny carvings on the bar came together to form one giant image of an apple tree against a cloudy sky. 'It's beautiful,' she said softly.

The man stared at her. For a moment, she worried that the translation field hadn't worked properly. The TARDIS supposedly enabled its occupants to speak and understand any language, even when they weren't nearby. But like everything else about the TARDIS, this was miraculous yet not entirely reliable. The man had presumably spoken to her in Welsh – had he heard her reply in English? If so, did he speak Victorian English? Maybe her modern South London twang had bamboozled him.

But then his weather-beaten face broke into a smile. 'Thank you very much,' he said, sitting down beside her. 'Name's Bergam.'

'I'm the Doctor,' the Doctor said. 'And this is –'

'Rose, yes,' Bergam said. 'Heard you the first time. Best forgive them . . .' He gestured at the other locals of the Charging Ram. 'Don't get many visitors these days.' He shot a wary look out of the window, watching the setting sun as though it were a dwindling bank balance.

A red-headed barmaid with old eyes approached with two steins, their contents frothing over the sides. She set them down before Rose and the Doctor.

'On me,' Bergam said, placing four coins on the bar. The woman snatched them up, nodded her thanks and hurried away.

'That's . . . kind of you,' Rose said doubtfully, looking down at the bitter-smelling liquid.

'Can't drink from the loch,' Bergam said. 'Too salty. And there's not much rainwater left in the well. This is all we have.'

'Much obliged,' said the Doctor, taking a cheerful swig. Rose knew he had two hearts, but she'd never thought to ask how many livers he had – or if he even had one.

Bergam sipped from his stein. The drink, whatever it was,

left foam in his moustache that bubbled like acid. 'So,' he said. 'What's your business in Lamond?'

The Doctor reached into his leather coat and produced a wallet. In Rose's opinion, this was the most useful thing the Doctor owned. The wallet contained a slip of blank paper that appeared to be a genuine identity document, with details plucked from the Doctor's mind and embellished by whoever was viewing it. If the psychic paper ever got wet, lost or destroyed, Rose and the Doctor would probably have to live out the rest of their days in a fourteenth-century Ottoman prison, or stuck in customs at Heathrow Airport.

The Doctor flipped open the wallet. 'We're from the department of . . .'

'Telephone pole inspectors,' Rose suggested.

'Exactly.' He showed the paper to Bergam.

'Te-le-phone?' Bergam repeated.

'Or telegraph,' the Doctor said.

'Either one,' Rose agreed.

'We check everything's up to code on behalf of . . . the Queen, I suppose,' the Doctor went on.

Bergam squinted. 'The *Queen* sent you here?'

'We took a wrong turn,' the Doctor said. 'On our way to Tyronica Prime.'

'Oh,' Bergam said, as though he might be familiar with the planet of the limb-swapping transhumanists. 'Rotten luck.'

'Not at all,' the Doctor said. 'We weren't in any hurry –'

'I didn't want to go at all,' Rose chimed in.

– 'and we like discovering new places,' the Doctor finished.

Bergam glanced around the bar and lowered his voice. 'Well, if you're wise, you won't stay long.'

Rose scanned his face for any hint of a threat, but Bergam looked uneasy rather than aggressive.

'Why's that, then?' she asked.

'It's not safe after dark. You can't leave now, but you should go at first light.' His shoulders sagged. 'I'd join you, if only I had anywhere else to go.'

Rose felt that tickling at the nape of her neck again. 'What happens after dark?'

Bergam leaned in, elbows on the bar, head bowed. 'You wouldn't believe me if I told you.'

'Try us,' the Doctor said quietly.

Bergam studied them both, then shrugged. 'All right. Don't say I didn't warn you.' He turned slightly on his stool. 'See that fetching woman in the grey cloak?'

Rose looked. The standards of beauty in nineteenth-century Wales might have been different from those of twenty-first-century London – the woman Bergam had pointed out was haggard-looking, with buck teeth and pockmarked skin. 'Who is she?'

'The blacksmith's wife. Or, she was – he burned his hand in the forge. The wound turned odorous, and then the sickness spread to his arm, then the rest of him. He was gone within days.'

Rose didn't do her A levels, but she knew enough biology to guess that Bergam was describing some kind of bacteria. She resisted the urge to enlighten him, though. If she tried to explain that the world was positively *covered* in tiny, invisible creatures that were mostly harmless until they gathered in sufficient numbers, she could end up in a madhouse, or burned as a witch, or something.

'That's awful,' she said instead.

'Not as awful as what happened when he came back,' Bergam replied.

The Devil's Seamstress

Rose wasn't sure she'd heard him correctly. 'Came *back*?'

'Aye.' Bergam stared down at the bar, as if he was hypnotised by the carved snakes. He ran a dirty finger over their wooden fangs. 'The blacksmith's wife saw her dead husband wandering through the forest at sunset.'

The hairs on Rose's arms stood up. 'Could it have been someone who just . . . looked like him?'

'See now, I had the very same thought. The blacksmith was six foot seven. If a tall traveller happened to be passing by, the widow could well have imagined the rest. Grief can play tricks on you – I know that better than anyone. After my father caught a chill and passed, I kept thinking I heard his voice, but it was only ever the wind.' He sipped his drink. 'Anyhow, the night after the widow saw the blacksmith, there was another sighting. The cooper, that fellow there . . .'

Bergam pointed at an ancient, bony man in breeches and a wool cap. Rose was pretty sure a cooper made barrels, or maybe horseshoes.

'He saw his son drinking from the well,' Bergam went on. 'The son he'd buried the week before, after he fell from a mare and broke his neck. Unlike the blacksmith's wife, the cooper got a good look, up close. He looked his dead son right in the eye.'

The wind moaned outside. The greasy curtains billowed, ragged ends scraping along the floor like long skirts. Rose tried to ignore the knot of dread growing in her stomach.

Above her head, the low ceiling creaked. She hadn't realised there was a second floor. Someone was up there, moving around.

Neither Bergam nor the Doctor seemed to hear the sound.

'So people are coming back from the dead?' the Doctor said.

'It's worse than that. Here's the thing.' Bergam stared down into his drink for a moment. 'The cooper said his lad had *grown*. From five foot one to well over six feet.'

'*That's* odd,' the Doctor said, as though everything up to this point had made perfect sense.

Bergam huffed. 'I know that look. You think we're daft country folk spinning tales. The cooper's nearing seventy. You think his eyes are probably failing, and his mind, too. Can't say I blame you. Didn't believe it myself – till it was my turn.' There was a wobble in his voice now.

'Who did you see?' Rose asked softly.

'My dad,' Bergam said. 'Recognised his hands. Big and rough – I'd been on the wrong end of them often enough. He still wore his wedding ring, too small to get over the knuckle. But he was taller than he should've been, and he wore another man's face. Horribly scarred, but I recognised it. The face of the cooper's son.'

The Doctor snapped his fingers. The sound was like a gunshot, making both Rose and Bergam jump.

'Do you mind?' Rose demanded.

'I remember now!' the Doctor said excitedly. 'The stories they tell in Lamond – stories they'll keep telling for generations. *The Patchwork Man.*'

Bergam shushed him and glanced around, as though it was dangerous to say the words. 'The very one,' he whispered.

'Who's the Patchwork Man?' Rose asked.

'He – *it* – is all the town's ghosts,' Bergam said. 'Stitched together by the devil's seamstress.'

A year ago, Rose would have dismissed this as impossible. Not now. 'When you saw this bloke,' she began, 'the tall man with the hands and the face – what did you do?'

'I ran.' Bergam wouldn't meet her gaze. 'I hid under my bed like I still had my milk teeth. The following day, five of us set out at sunrise to search the forest. We split up to cover more ground. And at sunset, only four returned.'

There was a sudden *gulp* from the cauldron. Rose turned to look. The blacksmith's wife prodded the logs beneath with an iron rod. Sparks skittered out across the floor, as though fleeing from the flames.

'What happened?' Rose asked.

'To Haisman? Still don't know. At daybreak, the four of us followed his trail, which ended in what Terrance called "an unremarkable copse". We spread out to keep looking and, well, this time, only three returned. Couldn't find hide nor hair of Boucher. After that, we decided to leave well enough alone. I was a coward, yet again.'

'There are worse things to be,' the Doctor said quietly.

Rose was nervous, but excited, too. This must be why the TARDIS had brought them here. Now the wandering-around bit of the adventure was over – it was time to move on to the helping-people part.

'Right,' she said. 'Let's start at the beginning. Was the blacksmith's wife the first person in town to see a ghost?'

'Aye.'

'And when was that, exactly?'

'Must be getting on three weeks ago now,' Bergam said.

'What year?'

She kept her voice casual, but Bergam was no help. 'This year, like I said. But that's only the first time *we* saw the ghost. I can't speak for that rich fellow in the manor in the valley.'

'Which manor?' the Doctor asked.

'You didn't pass it?' Bergam gestured out the window, though it had grown too dark to see anything. 'Great big house. Black ropes all leading to it, like it's a fly at the centre of a web.'

'Not ropes,' the Doctor said slowly. 'Power lines.'

'Who owns it?' asked Rose.

Bergam shrugged. 'Don't know his name. Never met him, though his servants sometimes come to town for supplies. Or they used to, before all this started. Anyway, he may know more.'

'He may indeed,' the Doctor said thoughtfully.

Rose still didn't want her drink, and she'd just thought of a use for it. 'Excuse me,' she said, standing up. Leaving the

Doctor to talk with Bergam, she made her way over to the pretty, dark-haired woman in the expensive dress.

'Would you like a drink?' she asked, holding out the mug.

The woman glanced at her and blinked slowly. 'No,' she said. 'Thank you.'

'How about you?' Rose offered the mug to the blonde girl in the plain dress, who shot her a silent look of alarm.

'I'll take that as a no.' Rose laughed easily. 'Can't say I blame you. To be honest, I'm not even sure what this is.'

The woman didn't return the smile. 'Metheglin, I believe.'

'What's that when it's at home?'

'Fermented honey. My fiancé's coachman is partial to it. Too partial, in my opinion. He insists that it cures ailments, and yet it seems to do nothing for his gout.' The woman said all this absently, like she wasn't even listening to herself. Her voice was quiet, her accent posh.

Rose took the empty seat on the rich woman's other side. 'I'm Rose.'

'Charmed,' the woman said automatically.

'Nice to meet you, Miss Charmed.'

The woman blinked, as though there had been a script for this conversation and she'd just realised a page was missing. She looked at Rose as though seeing her for the first time.

'I hope you don't mind my saying so,' the woman said, 'but to my eye, you don't appear to be a local.'

Rose looked down at her denim jacket and trainers. 'What tipped you off?'

'Are you perhaps –' the woman looked uncertain – 'Prussian?'

'Sure,' Rose said. 'Why not?'

The woman extended a hand, as if she expected Rose to kiss it. 'I'm Elspeth.'

Rose shook it instead. 'Rose.'

'You said.'

'Yeah, but I wasn't sure you were listening.'

The woman forced a smile. 'Forgive me. I'm terribly tired.'

Rose turned to the blonde girl. 'And you are?'

'My lady-in-waiting,' Elspeth said before the girl could reply.

The girl stood, curtsied and sat down again.

Rose had run out of ways to keep the conversation going. Fortunately, Elspeth had a follow-up: 'That man. Is he your husband?'

This was always an awkward question to answer. Rose struggled to explain, even to herself, how she could travel alongside a handsome, charming man like the Doctor without developing complicated feelings for him. But he had told her he was 900 years old, and though he hadn't specified whether that was Earth years or Gallifrey years – or dog years, or something else entirely – she knew she must seem very young to him. Also, she reminded herself firmly, *she had a boyfriend*.

'No,' she said, keeping it simple. 'He's just the Doctor.'

To Rose's surprise, the woman's eyes brimmed with tears.

'What's wrong?' she asked, alarmed.

'*I* was going to marry a doctor,' Elspeth said. 'Next week, in fact.'

Rose gasped. 'Oh no. What happened?'

She expected some ghastly story – another horse-riding accident, or an infected burn, or perhaps the woman's fiancé had drowned in the well. For all she knew, a war was happening, and he had been gored by a French bayonet, or something. But the woman responded with something much more banal: 'I don't know. I've been preparing the château for a month. Vincent was supposed to join me. But he never came.'

Rose had been stood up before. She supposed it was even more painful in a pre-mobile world when there was no hope of even an apologetic text – and when it was your fiancé.

'I'm so sorry.' She found herself matching the woman's posh accent. 'Men can be . . . heedless . . . of women's feelings.'

'Not Vincent,' Elspeth said. 'He was so noble, so kind. Something must have happened to him.'

Yeah, something like another woman, Rose thought.

'I sent a letter, but received no reply,' Elspeth continued. 'So I set out for his manor in person, but when I reached this village, they told me it was unsafe to go any further. That the forest is *haunted*.' She stared bleakly out of the window. 'Ordinarily, I would ignore such superstitions, of course. Vincent is a man of science, and he would have scoffed at such things. He would have tried to pass through the forest regardless.'

Perhaps that's why he's missing, Rose thought. The hairs on her arms stood up.

'Are you going to postpone the wedding?' she asked awkwardly.

Elspeth frowned. 'How?'

Right, Rose thought. *No mobiles*. The guests would all have been invited by letter and may already be on their way.

'Can you get back to your château?' she asked.

Elspeth nodded. 'The road in that direction is perfectly safe, or so I'm told. Certainly, I was not accosted on my journey here.'

'I think you should go,' Rose said, feeling protective of her new friend. 'The villagers are right – it's too dangerous to stay.'

Elspeth was silent for a long time. Then she said, 'I suppose I shall, come daybreak. May I offer you some advice in turn?'

'Sure,' Rose said, surprised.

Elspeth sniffled, dabbed away her tears with a silk handkerchief and took a deep, shuddering breath. 'Do not lose your doctor,' she said finally, 'as I have lost mine.'

Rose was about to reply when a terrible scream came from outside.

The Shrunken Pig

The Doctor and Rose reached the doorway at the same moment and got stuck as they both tried to run through at once. It would have been almost comical if not for the blood-curdling screech of horror that still echoed in the chill night air.

Finally, they burst through the curtains. Rose saw a woman near the well, crouching over what looked like a large sack of kindling. She had a bulbous nose and hair like matted straw, and was dressed in petticoats with muddy hems.

'Wynnie!' the woman shrieked.

Rose ran over and grabbed the woman's hand. Her flesh was deathly cold, and it seemed to tingle the same way Rose's neck had earlier.

'What's going on?' Rose demanded.

'It got Wynnie!' the woman wailed.

Rose's other hand fell on the sack, which had a curious, fuzzy texture. As her eyes adjusted to the dark, she realised it wasn't filled with kindling. In fact, it wasn't even a sack. It was some kind of animal, its furry skin stretched over brittle bones.

Rose snatched her hand away with a squeak of revulsion. 'What on Earth . . .?'

'My Wynnie,' the woman sobbed. 'What has it done to her?'

Rose saw the trotters sticking out from under the corpse and realised the animal was the brown pig with the white nose – and yet, it couldn't be. It had shrunk to half its size, and it was so thin.

The Doctor crouched beside her. 'Interesting.'

Not the word Rose would have chosen. 'Have you ever seen anything like this?' she asked.

'Steady on. I've only been here five seconds.' The Doctor buzzed his sonic screwdriver at the dead animal. Its teeth shone in the eerie glow.

'It looks like it starved to death,' Rose said.

'It didn't starve.' The Doctor checked the readout from the sonic. With his other hand, he palpated the creature's dried, flaky flesh. 'It died of thirst.'

Rose thought of dried pork jerky in little plastic wrappers at the supermarket. She felt ill. 'But *how*? We saw it when we arrived. It was fat and healthy –'

She broke off as she spotted something between the trees in the distance. A faint blue haze shimmered around it, like the fog had been tinted somehow, but it soon took the form of a man, well over six feet tall. The figure wore a pilgrim's hat, a cloak and giant riding boots. His face was hidden by shadow, but for two pinpricks of blue light.

The Patchwork Man, Rose thought.

As she looked into its eyes – she assumed they were eyes –

the air seemed to crackle. A deep chill swept over her. And then the apparition turned and began walking away.

Rose's paralysis broke, the air returning to her lungs. 'Look!' She grabbed the Doctor's shoulder and pointed frantically with her other hand. 'There!'

The Doctor looked up from the dead pig and spotted the retreating figure. He sprang to his feet. 'Stay here,' he commanded, sprinting towards the apparition.

'Sod off,' Rose cried and ran after him.

The Doctor raced across the muddy square and leapt over a low ramshackle fence, his leather coat flapping. Rose struggled to keep up on the uneven ground.

The figure had no trouble, crushing the brambles beneath his giant boots as he walked away. He didn't pass through things, like a ghost would – then again, the only ghosts Rose had ever met were actually aliens.

'Wait!' the Doctor shouted. 'We'd just like a chat!'

Only the Doctor would casually yell this while pursuing the undead. Incredibly, it worked. The figure stopped and slowly turned.

Rose skidded to a halt, her heart pounding. Shadows turned the man's face into a black void, except for the two glowing blue orbs.

'Phew,' the Doctor said. 'I wasn't sure you'd heard me.'

A rumbling voice came from the apparition. The words seemed malformed, as though the mouth that birthed them had too few or too many teeth.

'You – should – run,' it said disjointedly.

Actually, that sounded like quite a good idea to Rose. But

the Doctor stood firm. 'We *were* running,' he said reasonably. 'Tell me, what happened to that pig?'

The Patchwork Man moved towards them, boots thudding the dirt. The eyes glowed brighter and brighter. A meaty yet chemical odour crawled up Rose's nostrils.

She backed away. 'Doctor?' she said.

'What are you?' the Doctor asked curiously. 'That pig looked like it died of thirst, but *instantly*. Dehydration like that takes weeks.'

The apparition towered over them, reaching out with both hands. The flesh was grey except for pale-blue veins. Rose spotted the wedding ring on a finger, too small to fit over the knuckle.

The Doctor slowly reached into his pocket. 'It may *look* like I'm reaching for a weapon,' he said, 'but actually, I just want to do a quick scan.'

The creature lunged at him –

Rose screamed –

But then the giant's boot sank into a muddy puddle.

The creature let out a hiss of anger, or maybe pain, and leapt backwards out of the muck. That strange humming sound suddenly filled the air, getting louder and louder, so loud that it made Rose's teeth vibrate. She clamped her hands over her ears and squeezed her eyes shut, unable to think.

And then the noise stopped. Rose opened her eyes and looked around.

The creature was gone.

The Ancient Mariner

'What was that thing?' Rose demanded as she and the Doctor made their way round the clearing. She couldn't see any footprints or broken branches to indicate where the giant creature might have gone. They might have better luck in the daylight, but she wasn't counting on it.

The Doctor was buzzing his sonic at the ground as they walked. 'The Patchwork Man, I assume.'

'Yeah, thanks – I figured that part out on my own,' Rose said. 'But what *is* it?'

'I've no idea.' The Doctor rubbed his hands together. 'Fantastic.'

'You're nine hundred years old. You must have come across something like this before.'

'That's the great thing about the universe. No matter how much of it you've seen, there's always more. Don't you like surprises?'

'I like surprise parties,' Rose said. 'I like finding a surprise tenner in my pocket. I'm not so keen on surprise zombie ghosts. The Gelth were enough for me.'

'Well then, I have great news. That wasn't a Gelth, or a ghost, or a zombie.'

'Actually, I've changed my mind. I don't even like surprise parties.'

After a few more miserable minutes of poking around in the cold and the dark, they made their way back to the Charging Ram, where Bergam looked relieved to see them. He disappeared upstairs for a minute and offered them rooms for the night when he returned. To Rose's relief, the Doctor accepted.

Rose's room was a cramped space with a sloped ceiling, floral wallpaper and a small bed draped in a handmade quilt. A wooden chest at the foot of the bed contained extra blankets and a faint smell of dried flowers – too faint to displace the odour of the Patchwork Man, which still lingered in her nostrils. But she was grateful for the extra blankets. It was cold up here, away from the fire.

On the bedside table sat an oil lamp, already lit, the glass chimney smoky with years of use. The pewter base had also been engraved with apples and snakes.

Rose went over to draw the curtains, hoping to keep out the cold. She took one last look at the moonlit forest behind the tavern. The trees swayed gently in the night breeze, their leaves rustling. She hoped Elspeth's groom had simply abandoned her – but after seeing that *thing*, it seemed likely that something far worse had happened to him.

Rose pulled the curtains shut and turned to face the bed. She didn't usually get the chance to sleep during her adventures with the Doctor. The first time they'd met, he'd grabbed her hand and told her to run. It felt like she'd been running ever since.

Usually she'd watch some TV with her mum to wind down before bed. But since meeting Charles Dickens, she'd decided to read more books. A shelf in the corner contained two leather-bound volumes – the King James Bible and a book called *Lyrical Ballads*.

Rose turned down the Bible – things hadn't gotten *that* bad, not yet – and tossed the book of ballads on to the bed. Hopefully, it would calm her racing thoughts.

Slipping under the covers, she began reading by the lamplight. The book began with *The Rime of the Ancient Mariner*, which Rose was vaguely aware of but had never read. In the poem, a wedding guest was harangued by an old sailor who claimed to have been led safely through Antarctic ice by a bird, which he then shot with a crossbow, cursing himself and his crew.

Halfway through the poem, Rose's eyelids grew heavy. She drifted off to sleep, the book still open on her chest. She dreamed she was on a boat, surrounded by a crew all dead of thirst. Until they rose to their feet before her eyes.

The early bedtimes of the pre-light-bulb era led to early mornings. Rose was awoken at dawn by the sound of stable doors creaking, horses snuffling and carriage wheels clattering. She dressed quickly and hurried downstairs. The tavern was empty, the fire cold. She walked out on to the street in time to see Elspeth, the rich young woman, climbing the steps into a carriage. Her lady-in-waiting fussed around her.

'You're leaving,' Rose said, relieved.

Elspeth turned. Her subtle makeup was perfect, but her eyes were puffy. 'I am,' she said. 'You were right, Rose. It is not safe for me to stay.' She gazed out across the hovels of the little town. 'I keep thinking, what if Vincent arrived at the château after I left? What if something befalls me here, and he is left waiting for me, as I have waited for him?'

It was hard to tell her the truth, but Rose knew these were the moments when the truth was most important. 'I don't think he's coming back,' she said.

'You do not know my Vincent. He is a brilliant man. He will find a way – and next week, we shall be married.' But Elspeth's red-rimmed eyes suggested that she didn't quite believe it, either. 'Farewell, Miss Rose.' She bowed her head and slipped into the carriage.

Her lady-in-waiting followed and closed the door. The driver whipped the horses, and the carriage rattled away up the muddy street.

The Doctor appeared behind Rose. 'Sleep all right?' he asked.

Rose stretched her stiff neck. She knew she'd had unsettling dreams, but couldn't remember any details. 'Fine,' she lied. 'You?'

'Never been a fan of hotels, to be honest. I'm more of a camper. But the breakfast was good. I give it five stars – or I will in a couple of centuries, when online reviews are invented. Got you this.'

He threw her a ball wrapped in stained cheesecloth. It felt warm.

'What is it?' Rose asked as she unwrapped it.

'Breakfast. Five stars, like I said.'

Rose peered dubiously at the contents. 'Is it a . . . baked potato?'

'You know what? I didn't ask. Come on.'

They left the town the same way they'd entered it, and soon they were back on the dirt road.

'Where are we going?' Rose asked.

'Following the power lines. To the manor owned by the mysterious rich gentleman.'

'What if the Patchwork Man *is* the mysterious rich gentleman?'

'Ooh, that would be a good twist – mind your step.' The Doctor pointed to a puddle as they passed it.

Rose took a bite out of the potato and grimaced. 'You know, in France, a potato is called an "apple of the soil"?' she said, her mouth full. 'This is the first time I've ever understood why.'

'Oh, come on. A bit of ketchup and some grated cheddar, and that would be delicious.'

'I agree, but do you see either of those ingredients on it? Because I sure can't taste them.'

After almost two hours of walking – and whistling, in the Doctor's case – Rose's feet were getting sore, and her sweaty armpits were chafing. 'We should have taken the TARDIS,' she puffed.

'Too risky. We might land in the wrong –' The Doctor cut himself off, but it was too late.

'Aha!' Rose crowed. 'So you admit you have no idea how to fly it.'

'I know perfectly well how to fly her,' the Doctor said defensively. 'It's just that she also likes to steer herself occasionally. It's less like driving a car and more like riding a horse.'

'To me, that sounds like the key disadvantage of horses,' Rose said. 'It might even be the reason we invented cars. And *don't* –' she held up a hand – 'launch into an anecdote about that time you met Henry Ford or Mr Volkswagen. I'm not in the mood.'

'Actually, Ford invented the production line, not the car,' the Doctor replied. 'Remarkably boring man. Didn't say any of the clever things people think he said. Have you never ridden a horse?'

'Once,' Rose grumbled. 'It was awful.' She had visited Tadworth with Jackie when she was fourteen, and once on a horse had spent the entire time holding on to the reins for dear life, even though the animal never even got to a trot. Going downhill had been especially terrifying.

'You just haven't met the right horse, then,' the Doctor said. 'Don't worry, we'll sort you out before we leave.'

'I don't want to be "sorted out",' Rose protested, but the Doctor had stopped listening. He had spotted one of the power poles and stared up as they passed it. 'That's a sizeable transformer,' he observed. 'We must be getting close.'

'Impressive deduction,' Rose said, pointing to a rambling manor nestled in the valley about a kilometre away.

'Oh! Well spotted, Rose.'

The manor was protected by a stone wall and a wrought-iron gate. Smoke corkscrewed upward from one of several chimneys. The power lines led directly to the roof. Rose could see other power poles around it, with cables stretching in every direction. The house was just as Bergam had described, like a spider at the centre of a web.

The Doctor ignored the house, looking at the other side of the valley. 'Oh, that's clever.'

Rose was puffing from the uphill climb, her breath making clouds in front of her. 'What is?'

'Lightning rods.' The Doctor pointed to the spikes on each of the surrounding hilltops. 'There, there and there – we're well before solar panels, or any kind of grid, but if you collect enough lightning, you could keep a sizeable battery charged.'

'No carbon gets out, I guess,' Rose said.

'Sometimes it's what gets *in* that you have to worry about.'

'What's that supposed to mean?'

The Doctor didn't seem to hear her. He peered down at the manor. 'Let's have a chat with the renewable energy enthusiast, shall we?'

'Do you think he'll have cheese or ketchup?' Rose asked hopefully.

'He might even have an induction hob.'

Rose took a breath and started walking down a narrow animal trail. It was less exhausting than the uphill trek had been, but she kept tripping on hidden tree roots and rocks. 'Why would he run his house off a battery?

I wouldn't have thought people knew about climate change before the twentieth century.'

'You'd be wrong. Eunice Newton Foote mentioned it to me during a game of table tennis in 1886,' the Doctor said from behind her.

Rose rolled her eyes. 'Okay, but surely a "renewable energy enthusiast" would have invented an electric heater or something, rather than a fireplace?'

The Doctor frowned at the smoke above the manor. 'Excellent point. Which is just what I said to Eunice after I lost the rematch – Rose!'

He grabbed the back of her denim jacket just as Rose's foot hit the earth and kept going. What had looked like solid ground was a hole filled with water and covered with leaves. Rose's foot went ankle-deep, and a violent chill flashed up her spine before the Doctor yanked her back on to solid ground.

'Ugh.' Rose looked down at her ruined shoe. 'Just once, could we go somewhere warm and dry?'

'We visited that Venusian city inside the volcano,' the Doctor protested.

'I said "warm". Something *in between* freezing cold and scorching hot.'

'All right, Goldilocks.' The Doctor flicked at Rose's blonde hair, then crouched over the hole. 'This doesn't look like a naturally occurring sinkhole, does it?'

Rose looked around, and her skin crawled. 'Um, Doctor?'

'Perhaps an animal?' the Doctor mused. 'But it would have to be something big to dig a burrow of this size.'

'Doctor!' Rose squeaked.

Her tone made him look up. He noticed the headstone at one end of the long, rectangular hole.

'Oh.' He squinted at the engraving. 'Eighteen thirty-eight. And the headstone is about . . .' He sniffed the top of it. 'A month old, I'd say.'

Rose pointed. 'Are you going to sniff them all?'

The Doctor turned. As the wind picked up and carried the fog away, hundreds more headstones were revealed. They'd reached a cemetery.

Rose had always found cemeteries to be sad rather than spooky, but she wondered if the Doctor felt the same way. To him, these people weren't gone – he could pop into the TARDIS, zip back in time and visit them if he so chose. He'd also travelled to the furthest reaches of the future, which was a cemetery of a different kind. A place where everyone he'd ever helped was reduced to dust.

Rose was distracted from these gloomy thoughts when she saw that about a dozen graves were open.

Her skin crawled. 'Are vampires real? And are they fit, like in films?'

'Depends on the vampire – but either way, they're not as common as grave-robbers.' The Doctor made his way through the maze of headstones. 'Look at the dates. The older graves are undisturbed. Only the new ones are open.'

'Meaning what?' Rose asked.

'Whoever dug up these graves wasn't after gold or jewels.

They wanted the actual corpses, and they wanted them fresh.'

Rose shuddered. 'Let's find another way round.' She turned to walk back up the hill . . .

Only to find the trail blocked by the Patchwork Man.

The Bloodshot Eye

'Doctor!' Rose backed away, nearly falling into one of the open graves.

The Doctor spun round and spotted the figure, who was now ten or fifteen metres away. 'Oh, hello again!' He gave a cheery wave.

The Patchwork Man said nothing. His face was mostly concealed by his hat and his turned-up collar, but Rose could still see a single bloodshot eye. In the daylight, it didn't glow, but it was still a piercing shade of blue, surrounded by sickly pale skin. Even at this distance, he smelled like one of her mum's Christmas hams – in February.

'I told you,' he rasped, 'to leave.'

'We're just leaving now,' Rose said. 'Aren't we, Doctor?'

The Patchwork Man drew closer, fog swirling around his muddy riding boots. The wind caught his collar, exposing a line of ragged stitches across his throat. A horrifying realisation dawned on Rose as he walked past one of the open graves.

The face of the cooper's son. The hands of Bergam's father. The tall frame of the blacksmith's husband.

All the town's ghosts. Stitched together by the devil's seamstress.

Or by a grave-robber.

She could see by the Doctor's dark expression that he had reached the same conclusion.

'You didn't seem to like it when you stepped in that puddle,' the Doctor said. 'Why?'

'Because he's not a five-year-old,' Rose hissed, tugging at the Doctor's sleeve. 'Come on!'

'*They* didn't like it,' the Patchwork Man corrected, walking closer.

'I see,' the Doctor said. 'And who are *They*?'

'I keep Them fed in exchange for autonomy. This I use to hunt the loved ones of the Doctor.'

A shroud of dread settled over Rose. 'Have you met this guy before?' she whispered.

'No,' the Doctor said, staring at the approaching creature. 'But that doesn't mean he hasn't met me.'

It took Rose a second to understand his meaning. The life of a time traveller was complicated. Things didn't always happen to him in the correct order.

'They will be denied no longer,' the Patchwork Man said, reaching into his coat.

'Tell me,' the Doctor called. 'When we crossed paths before, did I look like this?' He gestured to his face. 'Did I have a long scarf, perhaps? Or –'

The Patchwork Man pulled out a crossbow.

Rose ducked just in time. There was a twang like a guitar string snapping, and she felt the displaced air as a sharp bolt flew overhead, almost close enough to graze her scalp.

'Run!' the Doctor yelled, like she wasn't already planning to do that.

They fled deeper into the cemetery, dodging headstones and leaping over open graves, Rose's wet shoe squelching. She heard the ratcheting of the crossbow and then another twang. This time, she saw the steel bolt as it flashed past. It hit a nearby headstone with enough force to crumble off a chunk. There was a little explosion of blue sparks.

As they ran, Rose risked a glance back. The giant was following them, mighty boots thumping the dirt. He didn't even have to run. His long stride meant he could easily step over the graves and keep up with his prey at a brisk walk.

He finished slotting another bolt into the crossbow and trained it on Rose. She threw herself sideways. The bolt slashed through the sleeve of her favourite denim jacket.

'Oi!' she cried.

They reached the edge of the graveyard and ran down another trail, worming into the forest. This time, the ground was rocky rather than muddy. If Rose twisted an ankle, they'd never get away. Even if she didn't, the Patchwork Man would have no trouble chasing them down. Rose looked frantically around for somewhere to hide.

There! A gap between two thick shrubs. Rose yanked the Doctor sideways off the trail, and they both tumbled to the ground, hidden by the tangled branches. Rose scooped up a stone about the size of a billiard ball. It wasn't much of a weapon — she was bringing a stone to a crossbow fight — but nothing else was available.

'Don't,' the Doctor whispered. He abhorred weapons of all kinds.

Rose shushed him.

'I mean it.'

The Patchwork Man was climbing the hill, buckles jingling on his belt. Rose clenched her teeth, hoping he'd walk right past.

He didn't. He stopped next to the bushes. She could hear him sniffing the air. Could he smell them over his *own* ghastly stench?

Thinking quickly, Rose flung the stone. Not at the Patchwork Man, but further along the trail. It crashed down noisily somewhere in the distance. The creature grunted and broke into a run. His boots thudded away towards the sound.

Soon, all was still.

After a minute, the Doctor said, 'I'm glad you didn't hit him.'

'I should've,' Rose hissed. 'He said he was *hunting your loved ones*. Who is he?'

The Doctor shrugged. 'No idea. If you spend two thousand years helping people, you make lots of friends and a handful of enemies. The enemies don't like introducing themselves over and over.'

'Two thousand years? I thought you were nine hundred.'

'I am, but I'll be two thousand eventually. The party is at Edinburgh Castle in 2039. Adele shows up to sing "Happy Birthday".'

Rose looked blankly at him.

The Doctor sighed. 'Right – 2005. Not there yet . . .' He poked his head out of the bushes. 'We should keep moving.

We're almost at the house, and whoever lives there is likely to be friendlier, statistically.'

'Firstly, low bar. Secondly, how do you know *he* doesn't live there?!'

'Didn't you smell him?' the Doctor asked. 'That's not a man who owns a bathtub, or even a change of clothes. The TARDIS brought us here for a reason. Maybe someone in that house needs our help.'

'If the TARDIS wanted us to go to that house, why didn't it land closer to it, or even inside?'

'She's very polite, you know. Doesn't like startling people.'

Rose rubbed her face. The Doctor was right. *Someone* lived in that manor – someone using technology ahead of their time. She and the Doctor had to get there, not just to solve the mystery, but to warn the occupant that there was a giant maniac outside with a crossbow.

'All right.' She thought of the smoke from the chimney. At least she'd be able to dry her shoe.

They emerged from the bushes and started to creep down the path.

'This is the same way he went,' Rose whispered. 'What if we bump into him again?'

'Good point.' The Doctor pointed to a narrow animal trail, which split off from the main one. 'Let's go that way.'

Rose nodded. She was about to enter the path when the Doctor said, 'Wait. Do you hear that?'

Rose closed her eyes and listened. There was a faint, high-pitched hum in the air. 'Yeah. I heard something like it earlier actually, but it was deeper.'

The Doctor frowned. 'You didn't mention that.'

Rose shrugged. 'I wasn't sure it was important.'

'*Everything's* important.'

Rose wanted to protest – the Doctor regularly mocked humans for caring about supposedly insignificant things – but he was already waving his sonic screwdriver around. Soon, the eerie blue glow fell on a small tin box, mounted on a stake in the shrubbery.

He thumbed a switch on the side of the screwdriver. The glow intensified. Something crackled inside the tin box. Sparks blasted out of the sides, the humming stopped . . .

And a tripwire appeared in front of Rose's legs. Like magic.

She gasped, stumbling backwards. 'I didn't even see that.'

'That's because it was invisible.' The Doctor pocketed the screwdriver and crouched next to the box. 'The current was bending the light round the wire, until I shut it off. Very clever indeed. Technology far ahead of this time.'

Rose looked around. 'What does it trigger?'

The Doctor shrugged, stepped over the wire and strolled up the trail.

'There might be more,' Rose said.

'I doubt it. Why would you put more than one trap on the same trail? Either the first one will get the victim, or they'll spot it and be very careful from then on.'

'Shouldn't *we* be careful?'

The Doctor grinned. 'Rose! It's like you don't even know me.'

The Negative Energy

The animal trail widened and eventually opened out near a two-metre stone wall, which surrounded the manor house. The wall looked ancient but it was covered with chicken wire, which looked new.

'What's the point of that?' the Doctor asked, studying the wire.

'Holds the wall together?' Rose suggested. 'I've seen that on cliffs in the Peak District. The council does it so rocks don't fall on to the road.'

'Makes sense on a cliff face,' the Doctor said thoughtfully, 'but not on a wall that is mortared together and nowhere near a road.'

Rose loved the Doctor's inquisitiveness, but her wet foot was getting cold. 'Can we keep moving?'

'In a minute.' The Doctor got his sonic screwdriver out of his pocket.

Rose grinned despite herself. 'One of these days, your curiosity is gonna get you into trouble.'

The Doctor grinned back. 'Well, it's lucky that I like trouble, isn't it?'

He pointed the sonic at the chicken wire and pushed the button. The device immediately flew out of his hand and stuck to the wall, about a metre off the ground. The buzzing sound stopped, and the little blue light went dark.

'That's never happened before,' he said, frowning.

Rose hadn't expected to be proven right quite so fast. 'Is the wall magnetic or something?'

The Doctor wasn't smiling any more. 'Not exactly.' He reached out and touched the sonic with his knuckles. When he didn't get electrocuted, he tried to pluck it off the wall.

'Can you get it off?' Rose asked.

'I'm trying.' The Doctor grabbed the device with both hands and put one foot against the stone wall to give him more strength. When the sonic still didn't budge, he lifted his other foot off the ground, too, putting all his weight into the attempt. He looked like an Olympic swimmer turning round at the end of a lane. But the sonic screwdriver remained stuck, almost like it had become part of the wall. The Doctor collapsed, puffing.

Rose was starting to feel alarmed. The Doctor had rescued them both from certain death with his sonic screwdriver, time and time again. He'd literally saved the world with it. What if they couldn't get it off this wall?

'Have you tried turning it off and then on again?' she suggested, a bit desperately.

'It *is* off.' The Doctor poked the button. 'And now it won't come back on. The negative charge has knocked it out cold.'

'Do you have a spare in the TARDIS?' Rose asked, trying to keep the panic out of her voice.

'A spare? *A spare?* It's not a tyre, Rose. It's an extraordinarily specialised scientific instrument. I only have –' he counted on his fingers – 'eight spares, and none of them are as good as this one. I can't just leave it here.' He gave another useless tug, then sighed and turned round.

'Doctor!' Rose cried.

'What is it?' the Doctor asked – except it wasn't the Doctor. It was a living skeleton, with skin so thin as to be semi-transparent. Cloudy eyeballs stared out of withered sockets. His teeth were long and yellow amid receding gums, and wisps of white hair sprouted from an otherwise bald skull.

Rose backed away. 'You – you're –'

'Oh!' The Doctor peered down at the backs of his suddenly bony hands. 'How did that happen?'

'What – how –' But as Rose watched, the Doctor became himself again, his flesh filling out, like a reinflated football.

'What just happened?' Rose demanded.

'The wire is charged with some sort of negative energy.' The Doctor turned back to the wall. 'Tried to suck the life force right out of me. If not for my second heart, it would have succeeded.'

'So it's another trap? Like the tripwire in the forest?'

'Yes, but not for us.' The Doctor put his hands on his hips. 'The Patchwork Man didn't like that puddle, did he?'

Rose didn't see the connection. 'So?'

'The oxygen atom in a water molecule has a negative charge, and if the water contains sodium – which the puddle would have, given the salty dirt around it – it can conduct electricity.'

'So this wall is like an extreme version of the puddle,' Rose said slowly. 'A much stronger negative charge.'

'Designed to suck the life out of the Patchwork Man. That'd be my guess. The fence will have an off-button somewhere. I'll just do a quick scan . . .' The Doctor reached into his pocket for the sonic screwdriver. Of course, the pocket was empty. 'Oh. Hmm, this could be a tricky one.'

'Whoever lives in the house probably set the trap, right? Let's just go in and ask where the button is.'

'And if he doesn't want to tell us?'

'I'll give him a very disapproving look,' Rose said. 'I'll channel my mother.'

The Doctor chuckled. 'Wow. I'm looking forward to seeing that. As long as I don't get slapped again.'

The Long, Brass Key

They must have set off in the wrong direction because by the time they found the gate they'd turned right four times, walking almost the entire length of the wall that encircled the grounds. It was mid-afternoon, and the winter sun was already descending towards the horizon.

Rose eyed the smoking chimneys of the manor a bit longingly. Travelling with the Doctor involved a lot of running and not much resting. She hoped there would be time to put her cold feet up in front of the fire.

Vicious spikes topped the wrought-iron gate. A rough rope dangled from a pulley next to it. The Doctor tugged on the rope, but Rose couldn't hear anything.

'I hate that,' she said.

'Hate what?' the Doctor asked.

'When you ring someone's doorbell but don't hear it ring. I always wonder, did it work? Is someone on their way? Do I try again and risk annoying them because they heard me the first time? Or do I stand here like an absolute lemon, *hoping* they did?'

'We could just let ourselves in.'

'We should give them at least a minute before we try,' Rose said.

The Doctor looked interested. 'Is that a human law?'

'Um . . .' Rose shrugged. 'More like etiquette, I suppose.'

'Like your five-second rule for food?'

Rose wrinkled her nose. 'I don't subscribe to that, but yes.'

'Smart,' the Doctor said. 'I don't think bacteria subscribe to it, either. Tiny things play by different rules. Just ask a quantum physicist.'

As they waited, Rose studied the brass plaque mounted on the stone, the writing on which was worn away.

'Mr Frank Someone-or-other,' she read. 'No, wait – *Dr* Frank Someone-or-other.'

'A doctor, eh?' said the Doctor. 'I do hope he's not a know-it-all.'

Rose snorted. She was about to ring the bell again when a man came bursting through the front door. He looked about thirty, with curly brown hair gone frizzy in the damp, and he wore what would have been a rather dapper suit if the shirt were tucked in and the tie wasn't flapping over one shoulder. In one hand, he clutched a long, brass key.

'What are you doing?' he cried, sprinting towards them.

'We're telegraph pole inspectors,' the Doctor said, reaching for his psychic paper. 'May we –'

'Are you mad?' The man reached the gate and started frantically fiddling with the lock. His green eyes were wide, and there was spittle around his lips.

He's the one who looks mad, not us, Rose thought.

Finally, the man managed to get the gate unlocked. 'Get in! Quickly!'

Rose slipped through the gap, and the Doctor followed. The wild-eyed man locked the gate again, then fled back up the driveway towards the safety of the building without a backwards glance.

'Friendly chap,' the Doctor said. 'We could be anybody.'

Rose broke into a run after the man. 'Let's get into the house before he realises that, yeah?'

When he'd almost reached the front door of the manor, the man tripped on a rut in the driveway. He tumbled forward, arms outstretched, his fob watch and a few coins flying from his pockets. Just as he was about to land face down on the muddy gravel, the Doctor launched forward and caught him by the back of his braces. The man dangled for a second, then righted himself and kept running without so much as a 'thank you'.

Rose hurried after them both, but something made her glance back to where the man's belongings had tumbled from his pockets. Something gleamed on the ground – the brass key, half trodden into the mud.

'Wait!' Rose cried. 'You dropped the key to the gate!'

The man didn't seem to hear. He disappeared through the front door of the manor. The Doctor, right behind him, stopped in the doorway. 'Rose! Come on!'

Rose kept running, keen to get out of sight. She supposed that if the man needed to unlock the gate again, he could pick up the key on his way back – it wasn't going anywhere.

She reached the doorway and darted into the house. The door slammed closed behind her.

Silence fell over the driveway. Nothing moved. At first, the only sound was the distant chatter of birds and the faint patter of approaching rain. Then the birds fell silent, and an eerie hum filled the air.

The key twitched, casting ripples across the surface of a puddle.

The hum grew louder and louder.

The key flopped like a fish for a second or two and then started to slide slowly across the gravel, as though pulled on an invisible string.

Soon, the key reached the wrought-iron gates and slid slowly underneath. Finally, the hum cut out, and the key stopped moving.

A moment later it was scooped up by a giant, grey hand, with thin blue veins and a gold ring on one finger.

The Other Doctor

The house was a bit like the TARDIS in reverse – smaller on the inside. Perhaps the walls were thick but hollow, to make room for all the primitive electrical wiring. Nevertheless, a spiral staircase with an intricately carved banister had been squeezed into the foyer, curled round a large marble statue of a muscular man in sandals, his toga hanging open to reveal a hideously scarred stomach. The man had a triangular beard and determined eyes. A light bulb dangled from the ceiling on a long chain so that it appeared to float just above the statue's cupped palms.

'Prometheus,' the Doctor whispered.

'Friend of yours, I suppose?' Rose whispered back.

The Doctor looked at her like she was barmy. 'He's not *real*, Rose.'

She rolled her eyes. 'How silly of me. Aren't we a bit early for light bulbs?'

'Quite right. They're not supposed to be invented until the 1840s, and look how thin the filament is – well ahead of its time.' The Doctor looked around. 'Whoever's house this is, they don't live long enough to share their invention.'

Gilded portraits of serious-looking people covered the walls. One depicted a grouchy-looking man with a sharp nose, a pointed chin and eyes that seemed to follow Rose around the room. Another painting showed the man who had unlocked the gate for them, a little younger, much calmer, his hair combed, his shirt buttoned up to the throat, his green eyes crinkled at the edges with an innocent smile.

'I have returned safely,' the man announced, though Rose couldn't see anyone else around. Then he rounded on them. 'Who are you, and why have you taken leave of your senses? Do you not know of the being that haunts these woods?'

Rose cleared her throat. 'I'm Rose. This is –'

'How did you get past my snares?' the man demanded.

'*Your* snares?' Rose crossed her arms over her chest. 'That tripwire could have killed me!'

'Very impressive, actually,' the Doctor said. 'Photons usually ignore electromagnetism – how did you centralise so much current without a Faraday cage?'

The man's eyes grew wider. 'You're from the university?' he guessed. 'Here to enquire after my progress?'

The Doctor and Rose looked at each other.

Well, it's a better cover story than telegraph pole inspectors, she thought.

The Doctor must have reached the same conclusion. 'We are indeed,' he said, holding up his psychic paper.

The man produced some spectacles from his waistcoat and squinted at the paper. 'You're a doctor?' He sounded faintly disappointed. 'I had thought that endeavour of such significance might warrant the attendance of a professor, or even perhaps the Chancellor –'

'You should be glad he's here, trust me,' Rose said.

The man cleared his throat. 'Of course. Quite right. But I'm afraid there's not much to see. My experiment has gone . . . um . . .'

'Wrong?' Rose suggested.

'Those are the experiments you learn the most from,' the Doctor said wisely.

'Of that, I have no doubt,' the man said. 'But in this case, my experiment has quite literally gone.' He crossed the room and peered out of one of the windows. 'It, well . . . left.'

Rose was about to ask what he meant when a freckle-faced woman with muscular arms appeared at the top of the stairs. She wore a white pinafore and her red hair was concealed under a cap except for a single, disobedient curl. 'Are you quite safe, milord?'

'No,' the man said gloomily. 'None of us are.'

The woman nodded as though this made perfect sense. 'I shall draw a bath,' she said firmly.

'Not just now, Janine. But do tell my father I am back inside.'

'Very good, milord.' Janine hurried away up the stairs.

'My housekeeper.' The man rubbed his face with his palms. 'She thinks all problems can be solved with a bath.'

'Most can,' the Doctor said. 'At least according to my old pal, Archimedes.'

Rose would have *loved* a bath. She was muddy, sweaty and cold. Her wet foot felt like it was about to drop off.

Frankenstein and the Patchwork Man

The Doctor, as usual, was somehow immaculate. She'd never known him to bathe, shave or even change his clothes. It was as if the grime simply couldn't keep up with him.

He rubbed his hands together. 'So,' he said. 'Tell us more about this experiment. We've come to help.'

'Forgive me,' the man said. 'I confess that when I sent for a representative from the university, I was in a state of great excitement, almost a mania, in my eagerness to present my discovery. Now I fear that, in my hubris, I have doomed us all.' He tidied his hair, smoothed down his vest and extended a hand. 'Perhaps we can begin anew,' he said. 'Dr V. Frankenstein, at your service.'

The Damned Book

'Dr Frankenstein,' Rose repeated.

'Yes,' the man said.

'Your name is Dr V. Frankenstein.'

'That is what I said.'

Rose forced a smile. 'Excuse us for a moment.' Without waiting for a reply, she dragged the Doctor out of the foyer and into an adjacent sitting room, where a velvet chaise-longue rested on a thick rug in front of a crackling fire.

The Doctor dug the bag of jelly babies out of his pocket. 'Have you ever roasted a jelly baby? Almost as good as a marshmallow.'

Rose slapped the bag out of his hand. Jelly babies bounced away across the rug.

The Doctor sighed. 'Probably stale anyway. They've been in my pocket since the 1980s.'

Rose pointed a quivering finger back towards the foyer. 'That,' she hissed, 'is Dr Frankenstein.'

The Doctor looked unfazed. 'So he says.'

Rose remembered the empty graves. The ragged stitches.

Frankenstein and the Patchwork Man

The way the villagers had each recognised a different body part. 'And the Patchwork Man *is his monster*!'

'Our host sounds English,' the Doctor said thoughtfully. 'Isn't Dr Frankenstein supposed to be Swiss?'

Rose was on the verge of hysteria. 'He's supposed to be *fictional*.'

The Doctor winced. 'Keep it down. We don't want to offend him.'

'Offend him?! He doesn't exist! And unless the TARDIS can take us inside a book . . .' She paused. 'Can it?'

'I'm afraid not,' the Doctor said. 'The Freytag drive got broken when I last visited Ahab.'

'What about computers? Could someone have made a game based on the novel, and the TARDIS landed inside it, or something like that?'

The Doctor's brows shot up. 'Ooh! Good guess. You could be right.'

Rose looked around, as though the furniture might dissolve into a spray of zeros and ones. Everything seemed as solid as before, but that only made her increasingly uneasy. If a world that looked this real could be fake, then she would go mad.

The Doctor reached for his sonic screwdriver and found his pocket still empty. 'All right then,' he said. 'Only one way to find out.' He sat cross-legged on the floor and motioned for Rose to sit opposite.

'What are we doing?' she asked.

'Sit down and see.'

She did. The Doctor held up his hands, like he was surrendering. Rose copied him.

'Do you know pat-a-cake?' he asked.

'I'm sorry?'

The Doctor slapped her hands, and then his knees. 'Pat-a-cake, pat-a-cake, baker's man,' he recited. 'Bake me a cake as . . . Rose, you're not doing it.'

Okay, so I've already gone mad, she thought. 'Pat-a-cake, pat-a-cake,' she began.

They went through the nursery rhyme three times, gaining speed before the Doctor stopped. 'Nope,' he said. 'This is reality. If it were virtual, our voices would have slowly gone out of sync with our hands.'

Rose was flabbergasted. 'Really?'

'Of course. What did you think the rhyme was invented for? Adults rarely check that the world isn't a simulation, but children are very diligent about it.' The Doctor stood up, stretched, then sank into the chaise-longue. It was too low for him, almost leaving his knees up to his ears. He didn't seem to mind though, holding his hands out towards the fire.

'So how can we be trapped inside a story then?' Rose asked. 'This is bonkers.'

'If you do a little research,' the Doctor said, 'most fiction is based on fact, and most fact turns out to be fiction. Did I ever introduce you to Pinocchio? Now *there's* a lad who would have got on well with the transhumanists of Tyronica Prime.'

'So Frankenstein might be a true story?'

'Well, that's the thing. I've met Mary Shelley –'

'Let me guess.' Rose crossed her arms. 'She beat you at table tennis.'

'Of course not,' the Doctor said. 'It was Scrabble. But I don't remember her mentioning a real-life Victor Frankenstein. And remember the date on the headstone? We're near the end of the 1830s. Mary's book was published decades ago. It already exists.'

'That damned book,' said a voice from behind Rose, and she almost leapt out of her skin.

She whirled round. An old man with bloodshot eyes and sagging grey skin loomed in the doorway. He wore faded flannel pyjamas and an old-fashioned nightcap, the pom-pom dangling over his bushy brows. Despite this, Rose recognised him from his grouchy portrait in the foyer.

'I bought a copy for my son on the occasion of his fourteenth birthday,' the old man said. 'I hadn't read it myself; I only knew it was about a scientist named Victor Frankenstein. My boy is called Vincent Frankenstein, and he'd expressed an interest in the sciences, so I thought he'd be amused by the coincidence.' He gave a deep, rattling sigh. 'More fool me.'

Dr V. Frankenstein, Rose thought. *Vincent. Not Victor.*

'Did he not like it?' The Doctor looked surprised. 'I thought it was fantastic.'

'Oh, he liked it all right,' the old man said. 'Read it over and over. Next thing I know, he's writing to universities, attending lectures. Wasting his title and my fortune on some cock-and-bull scheme to *create life*. I told him: "Vincent, creating life is a woman's job. A man's role is to *protect* it."

But he wouldn't listen.' Another grumbling sigh. 'My boy should have married Elspeth, fathered some sons and taught them to shoot by now.'

The pieces snapped together in Rose's mind. Elspeth's words in the Charging Ram – *Do not lose your doctor as I have lost mine*.

'We met her,' Rose said, in case the Doctor hadn't made the connection. 'She was preparing a château for after the wedding. She said it was next week.'

'Aye, indeed. And what preparation has my son done? None at all! He's been too busy playing with his scalpels and sewing needles.'

Rose thought of the stitches across the neck of the Patchwork Man and shuddered.

The old man coughed, thumped his chest with a hairy fist and spat a gob of phlegm into a brass vase by his feet. 'Anyway. Who the devil are you, and what are you doing in my house?'

The Doctor stuck his hands in his pockets. 'I'm the Doctor. This is Rose. We're here to help.'

'I told my damn fool son that I don't need any more doctors.'

'Well, lucky for you, I'm not that sort of doctor,' the Doctor said, with a smile that didn't quite reach his eyes.

'I'm fine!' the old man barked, and then exploded into a fit of coughing. Rose tried to pat him on the back, but he retreated, waving her away. 'I.' *Cough*. 'Am.' *Cough*. 'Fine.'

Rose suddenly remembered the monster had said something about 'hunting down all the loved ones of the Doctor'. Maybe he hadn't meant *her* Doctor. Maybe he had been referring to his creator, Dr Vincent Frankenstein.

'Father?' The man himself entered from the foyer, looking only marginally less frazzled. 'What are you doing out of bed?'

The old man caught his breath, and then said wheezily, 'You expect me to lie up there like an invalid while you invite more troublemakers into my home to worsen matters. I won't. I've a good mind to throw you all out and let the demon have at you.'

Vincent raised his hands in a placating way. 'Father, these are visitors from the university. They can help us.'

'When has a university ever helped anyone?' the old man sneered, stomping away up the stairs. The sounds of his coughs faded, and then a door slammed.

Vincent turned to the Doctor and Rose. 'Forgive him. He's not well.'

'What's wrong with him?' Rose asked.

'Some affliction of the heart. I listen to it, when he allows. It limps along, but quickly, like a three-legged mouse.'

'Heart trouble doesn't usually cause coughing,' the Doctor said gravely.

'That is a new symptom, troubling him for only a few weeks. He claims something in the air is to blame.'

'Hmm.' The Doctor reached for his sonic screwdriver and again found the pocket empty.

'I fear he is not long for this life,' Vincent said. 'But I am not ready to lose him. I need his wisdom, his guidance.' Seeing Rose's incredulous look, he added, 'Perhaps his wisdom was not evident from that conversation.'

'Perhaps,' Rose agreed.

'But please believe me when I tell you he *is* wise, and kind.'

'If you say so.' Rose had noticed that when men got scared, they looked for a bigger, older man to tell them what to do. Once they found him, they would downplay his flaws and project strengths on to him.

'So!' The Doctor clapped his hands together. 'Let's hear more about this experiment, then.'

Rose raised her hand. 'Actually, I'd like to get changed.'

'Forgive me!' Vincent looked horrified. 'What a poor host I have been thus far. Under normal circumstances, I would send the coachman to fetch your luggage, but I'm afraid . . .'

'Don't worry about it,' the Doctor said. 'We don't have luggage.'

Vincent gave them a subtle once-over, perhaps wondering for the first time how they had gotten to his doorstep with no car, horse, or whatever they used for transportation in the 1830s. A penny farthing, maybe? Rose made her expression as imperious as possible, hoping he would think it rude to ask.

It seemed to work. 'Some of my fiancée's clothes may fit you,' Vincent eventually said.

Rose tried not to be delighted, thinking of the fancy outfit she'd seen Elspeth in. 'Thank you very much,' she said.

Vincent reached for a bell-pull and tugged it. Rose couldn't hear a sound, but seconds later, the muscular young housekeeper appeared as if by magic.

That explained why the rooms seemed smaller than they should. The house must be full of hidden passageways, used by the servants to move invisibly from one end of the house to the other. Rose supposed that might have been a standard feature in the nineteenth century. For all she knew, it was a standard feature of rich people's houses in her time, too.

'Janine,' Vincent said. 'There are practical matters to attend to.'

'Shall I run a bath?' she asked hopefully.

'Yes,' Rose said. '*Please*.'

The Kind Master

The bathroom was large and elegant, with black and white floor tiles, a gilded mirror, and a mahogany dressing table against one wall, all gleaming under the candlelight from the sconces. A porcelain sink, white as bone, sat nestled within a vanity unit, though there was no sign of a tap. Rose guessed that running water wasn't yet common in this part of Wales, and yet the deep, claw-footed bathtub was filled with steaming liquid.

'This is my favourite room in the house,' Janine told her. 'I like the candles. Master Vincent – sorry, Dr Frankenstein – would've put those awful electric lights in here, too, but he says power and water don't mix.'

Rose leaned over the deep bath, inhaling the steam. 'Surely you didn't have to carry all this hot water up the stairs?'

Janine made a tinkling laugh. 'Oh no, miss. There's a dumb waiter in the corridor.'

Rose had seen a little square door in the corridor outside, with a crank. 'Is that one of those things where you put food in a box and then wind a handle to lift it to the next floor?'

'That's right, milady. I filled each bucket in the kitchen,

heated it over the fire, put it in the dumb waiter and gave the handle two-score turns. Then I climbed the stairs, took the bucket out and poured it into the bathtub.'

'How many buckets does it take to fill it?' Rose asked, aghast.

'A baker's dozen, miss,' Janine said matter-of-factly.

No wonder the young woman had the arms of a bodybuilder. Rose almost felt too guilty to climb into the bath now. But if she didn't, she would be wasting all of Janine's labour.

'Do you have to do everything yourself?' she asked.

'Goodness me, no. There's the coachman, and the cook, although Cook has gone to Newport to care for her father. And Dr Frankenstein insists on washing his own lab coat, though I've told him those stains won't depart without my expertise. He's worried the chemicals would be too harsh for my constitution, I suppose.' She huffed.

'How long have you worked for him?'

'Oh, I was born into it,' the housekeeper said proudly as she folded towels on a shelf near the bath. 'My mother served his father. My grandmother served his grandfather, my great-grandmother his great-grandfather, and so on back a hundred and fifty years.'

Rose thought this sounded like a curse. 'Didn't you ever want to do something else?'

'How do you mean, miss?'

Rose had met people from the past many times, but this was always the most jarring part, and she never got used to it. The telepathic field from the TARDIS could translate any language, but it couldn't translate culture. Sometimes, the things she heard seemed glaringly wrong, but she'd learned it could be dangerous to say so.

'Some day, with any luck, my daughter will care for his son,' the housekeeper went on. 'I hope she'll be as lucky with her master as I've been with mine. Dr Frankenstein needs so little, as he is always busy in his laboratory. Once the beds are made, the chamber pots are emptied and the clothes are washed, there's not much for me to do. I've even been teaching myself to read!'

'Good on you!' Rose smiled and squeezed Janine's shoulder. But the housekeeper stiffened, apparently unused to affection from nobles, so Rose let go again quickly. Not that she'd ever consider herself a noble.

'In the year without summer there were those awful storms,' Janine continued. 'Thunder crashing every night, crops failing, people eating their own horses just to stay alive. But Dr Frankenstein — of course, he wasn't Dr Frankenstein back then, just little master Vincent — always made sure me and mine were fed and warm.' She reached for Rose's denim jacket.

Rose shrank away. 'What are you doing?'

The housekeeper frowned. 'Undressing you, milady.'

'Oh, I can do that myself, thank you.'

'Very well.' The housekeeper stood back and waited.

They looked at each other for a moment. When the housekeeper still didn't leave, Rose said, 'Can I have some privacy?'

'Well, of course,' the housekeeper said. 'But . . . who will wash you?'

Rose allowed herself a moment to imagine having her feet scrubbed like she was a princess. She despised Vincent and history for taking advantage of this poor woman and all the others like her, but she had to admit it was hard to resist the temptation.

'I'll wash myself,' she finally concluded. 'Thanks, Janine. Perhaps you could go read a book?'

A puzzled smile crossed Janine's face. 'As you wish, milady. There's the bell-pull if you need.' She pointed to the contraption and slipped out of the door.

There didn't appear to be a lock, so Rose dragged a chair in front of the door, then undressed and sank gratefully into the bath. Something fragrant had been added to the water — lavender oil perhaps — and it was the most relaxed she'd felt in days.

Look at that, she thought. *There's a day spa after all.*

The Drunken Coachman

The housekeeper had left out a selection of clothes belonging to Vincent's fiancée. There were bonnets and bustles, corsets and capes. The items looked about the right size, but it was hard to work out how to put them on, especially since Rose refused to call the housekeeper back to help. Eventually, she managed to wriggle into a voluminous bell-shaped skirt and a linen top with sloped shoulders, which she covered with a paisley shawl. There was a pair of surprisingly modern boots with elastic sides, the kind Rose's mum always called 'Beatle boots'. When she pulled them on, Rose couldn't work out whether she had them on the correct feet. No matter which way around they were, they always felt wrong. It took her a while to realise they were identical. Had nineteenth-century people never noticed their left and right feet were differently shaped?

Still. Rose admired herself in the mirror. She looked glamorous, and felt it, too.

When she emerged from the bathroom, she noticed a painting leaning against the floor in the corridor. It depicted Vincent and Elspeth, holding hands. Presumably, the frame would grace a wall only after the couple were married.

As with most old portraits, neither of the subjects was smiling – but both looked like they were trying not to. Rose remembered how deeply in love Elspeth had seemed at the tavern. Perhaps there were more important things to deal with, but Rose hoped she and the Doctor could reunite the couple before they left.

Then again, she remembered the Doctor's words: *Whoever's house this is, they don't live long enough to share their invention.*

A big man in a long cloak was waiting at the bottom of the stairs. She flinched, thinking it was Frankenstein's monster – but no, the man's mutton-chopped face was a healthy colour. Too healthy, perhaps. He swayed a little on his feet. From the top of the staircase, Rose had a good view of his bald spot.

'Hello,' she said cautiously.

The man looked her up and down, and simply nodded.

'I'm Rose,' she tried.

The man nodded again.

She would have to be more direct. 'Who are you?'

'Coachman.' His voice was a rough grunt.

Rose remembered the housekeeper mentioning a coachman. 'Ah.'

'You've borrowed Miss Elspeth's clothes,' he said, a bit accusingly.

'You're drunk,' Rose countered.

The coachman squinted. 'And now you've borrowed her words, too.' He pointed a wavering finger at her. 'I had a bottle of scotch in the shed, and now it's missing. Are you the one who took it?'

'You think I'm going through sheds looking for booze?'

Rose remembered what Elspeth had said about the coachman, his fondness for metheglin, and his gout.

The coachman scraped his heel on the floor and examined it. 'Can't go anywhere,' he muttered. 'Not with that *thing* about.'

'You've seen it, then?' Rose asked.

'I was a soldier, once.' She wasn't sure he'd heard her. 'Fought at Navarino. Saw my friends blown apart by Egyptian cannonballs. Thought that was the worst thing that could happen to a man. Now I know – getting put back together is worse. Anyway.' He seemed to return to reality. 'The horses are chewing up the stables. Going mad with boredom.'

Not just them, Rose thought. 'You think it's wise to get sozzled while there's a monster lurking outside?'

'The comparative wisdom of sobriety,' the coachman enunciated carefully, 'eludes me.'

'I can see that.'

The coachman stared at the statue of Prometheus as he talked, as though he were speaking to the Titan rather than to Rose. 'Been eight years since Dr Frankenstein – just Master Vincent, back then – walked into the Charging Ram, introduced himself and asked if I knew how to shoe a horse. Seen plenty of things since. He sends me on the strangest errands. "Coachman, we need copper wire." "Coachman, we need sewing needles." "Coachman, we're going to the cemetery. Bring two shovels."' He shook his head and swayed a little on his feet. 'But this? It takes the biscuit. I tell you, if I'd known what he was going to put me through, I would have told him to clear off and find someone else to shoe his damn horse.'

'Do you live in Lamond?'

He shook his head. 'Here. Used to go down for a pint from time to time. No more.' He rubbed his face on his forearm. 'No more!'

Rose was getting uneasy. 'Where's the Doctor? *My* Doctor.'

The man's grey eyes widened, and he backed away from the bottom of the staircase. 'You're sick?'

'No,' Rose said quickly. 'I just came here with him. Leather coat, Northern accent, big ears.'

The coachman's stiff posture slackened. 'Oh. *That* fellow. Followed Dr Frankenstein into the laboratory.'

'And where is the laboratory?' Rose asked patiently.

The coachman jerked a thumb. 'That way.' He went to tip his hat, then seemed to realise he wasn't wearing one.

Rose descended the stairs and turned in the direction he'd pointed.

'Miss?' the coachman said.

Rose turned. 'Yes?'

'If you'll take my advice, you and the big-eared chap won't stay long.'

'Why's that?' she asked. 'Besides the obvious.'

'Can't you feel it?' the coachman asked.

Rose looked around. 'Feel what?'

His Adam's apple bobbed. 'Sometimes it helps to close your eyes.'

Uneasily, Rose did. At first, she heard nothing. Maybe the drunken coachman was talking nonsense. But after she'd stood motionless for a moment, she felt a faint tingling in her toes, which then zipped up the backs of her legs and up her spine, eventually reaching the fillings in her molars, where it became a deep, bass *hum*. It was similar to the sound she'd noticed in the forest, but much louder – no, more forceful. Like the sound was coming from here, in this house.

'What *is* that?' she asked.

The coachman didn't reply. When she opened her eyes, he was gone.

The Madman's Laboratory

Rose found Vincent's laboratory on the ground floor in the east wing of the manor. It had a chequered floor with drains in the corners, and two gleaming stainless-steel workbenches running parallel. She ducked under a hanging tray, wrinkling her nose against the smell of pickling liquid.

'Unfortunately, Shelley's book didn't go into much technical detail,' Vincent was explaining as he lifted a lab coat off a hook and pulled it on. 'So I had to improvise.'

'That's probably because it was made-up,' Rose said.

Vincent turned round, and saw her in his fiancée's clothes. A great sadness filled his eyes, but he simply harrumphed and said, 'Quite a good fit.'

The Doctor raised an eyebrow. 'Looking fancy, Rose Tyler.'

She attempted an ironic curtsy, but wasn't sure she'd pulled it off. 'What are you blokes up to, then?'

'Dr Frankenstein was explaining the particulars of his experiment.'

'Yes.' Vincent gestured to six hexagonal power points on one wall. 'I placed lightning rods on several nearby hilltops and connected them with a web of cables, which I kept off the ground using a matrix of poles. "Power poles", if you will.'

'Fascinating,' the Doctor murmured.

'The energy flowed out of these six points – "power points" – and was captured in a crown of cups, which was here –' he put his palms flat on the workbench – 'but I've since moved it to the basement. Over here . . .' He swept a hand across a row of giant bottles. 'I couldn't use formaldehyde to preserve the tissue samples, because my creation would have been poisoned before he took his first breath. So I devised a compound called tricophenylaldehyde –'

'Tissue samples?' Rose interrupted. 'You mean the bodies from the cemetery.'

'Science leaves little room for squeamishness,' Vincent said, a bit testily.

Rose wasn't squeamish. She'd seen things that would make Vincent's head spin. 'Does it leave room for the dignity of the dead?'

'There is no dignity in death,' Vincent snapped. 'It's a hideous process, to be avoided at any cost – and the grave-robber is an essential precursor to the physician.' He took a deep breath. 'I took limbs mostly from Lamond, where the people are of hardy stock and well-accustomed to exertion. I found their musculature superior. But the two lobes of the brain were taken from Lords Tagent and Jennery, both killed in a duel over Tagent's scorning of Jennery's sister.'

Rose raised an eyebrow. 'You figured the brains of the rich would be superior to those of the poor?'

Vincent nodded vigorously. 'Precisely.' Oblivious to her incredulous stare, he pointed to another bottle. 'Here I have a concentrated perfluorocarbon, for oxygenating blood. And this is chlorofluorane, with which I attempted to sedate my creation. I'm afraid I was . . . unsuccessful.'

'Really?' The Doctor stroked his chin. 'Usually, that stuff would knock out an elephant.'

'Well, he must have the strength of two elephants. He grabbed my assistant, Harold, and . . .'

'What happened?' Rose asked.

'I'm at a loss to explain it. Harold's body . . . shrivelled up.'

'Shrivelled,' Rose repeated.

'Like a raisin.' Vincent wouldn't meet her gaze. 'His screams will haunt me for the rest of my days.'

Rose remembered the pig, transformed into a shrunken skin-sack of bones. She glanced at the Doctor, trying to gauge his reaction. His mouth was a hard line.

'And then?' he said.

'And I – I ran. The creature escaped out of that window.' Vincent gestured to a barred window, where rain spattered on to the glass. Rose guessed that the bars were new – but that a creature with the strength of two elephants would have no trouble breaking through.

'When you read Shelley's book,' she said, 'didn't it seem like a cautionary tale? Like, maybe the point was that making monsters from bits of dead people isn't a good idea?' Rose hadn't actually read the book herself, but she thought she knew the broad strokes of the story: a bunch of people die because of an arrogant scientist playing God.

It was basically *Jurassic Park*, but with a zombie instead of a T.rex.

Vincent closed his eyes. 'In truth, I only feared that it might be impossible. My parents had a long, happy marriage until my mother succumbed to consumption last year, and . . .'

Rose's jaw dropped, picturing Vincent's mother being *eaten*, but the Doctor quickly nudged her. 'Tuberculosis,' he whispered.

'My father's heart began to give out as soon as she was gone,' Vincent went on. 'Theirs was the kind of union I long to have with Elspeth. She's at Loch Lamond right now, preparing the château for our wedding. I'm supposed to be there myself, but the creature has me trapped. I need my father to teach me how to be a husband and how to raise my children, yet I fear he'll be gone by the time Elspeth and I are wed. This experiment —' he gestured at the jars of chemicals on the workbench – 'was just the first step. I hoped to master the science of life and death, so I need never lose my father.'

Rose was hit by a wave of unexpected sympathy for the barmy scientist. She knew all too well how it felt to lose a father and the crazy lengths someone might go to in order to prevent it.

'The folly of my endeavours became clear to me the instant the creature sat up,' Vincent went on. 'But by then it was too late. Now he wants revenge.'

'Revenge?' Rose asked. 'For what?'

'A few days after the monster fled, a letter was delivered to my doorstep.' Vincent reached into his vest and produced a stained, torn envelope.

Rose took it and pulled out the letter inside. The words were smudged and clumsily written, as if the author's hands were too big for the quill. But the words were clear enough:

'You have made me an abomination,' she read. 'All who look upon my visage flee in terror. I will spend the term of my unnatural life alone. I shall ensure you do the same.'

'Sounds like he's read the book, too,' the Doctor said quietly.

'I filled the forest with snares,' Vincent said. 'I locked the gates and barred the doors to protect Janine and my father. I wrapped the outer wall in chicken wire and created a current of negative energy –'

'We're aware,' the Doctor said, looking annoyed.

'Was the idea to electrocute the creature if it tried to climb the wall?' Rose asked.

'Quite the opposite,' Vincent said. 'If it touched the wires, I had hoped the vital spark would be drawn *from* it, leaving the creature inert once more.' He pinched the bridge of his nose. 'A waste of time, as events transpired. Somehow, the creature is more intelligent than the noblemen from whose brains its mind was forged.'

Rose suspected this was more true than Vincent knew. Unlike him, she had little respect for the rich idiots who died duelling each other. And when she'd met the creature, it had seemed to radiate fierce cunning.

'I have no way of warning my beloved,' Vincent continued. 'She's at the château, heedless of the danger and utterly undefended. If the creature discovers she's not here, he will surely hunt her down.' He took a shuddering breath. 'My father is right. I have doomed us all, and Elspeth most especially.'

A lump of guilt formed in the pit of Rose's stomach. She had told Elspeth to go back to the château, when she might actually have been safer remaining at the Charging Ram. Rose couldn't have known that she was sending Elspeth to her death, but that didn't change the basic facts.

The Doctor had saved a lot of people, but not everyone. Rose thought often of those who hadn't made it. Wilson, the caretaker at Henrik's. Gwyneth, the clairvoyant at the funeral parlour. Raffalo, the mechanic on Platform One, and Suki, the journalist on Satellite 5. Her father, most of all.

Vincent had made a stupid mistake. But Rose wouldn't let him, or his fiancée, die for it.

'We can help you,' she said firmly. 'And Elspeth. Right, Doctor?'

The Doctor, as practical as ever, was examining a giant copper coil in a nest of cables up one end of the workbench. 'This is how your equipment was arranged on the day of the experiment?'

'Yes,' Vincent said. 'Why?'

'I can't figure out how it worked.'

Vincent wiped his eyes and pointed. 'Well, the current flowed –'

'I can see how it was *supposed* to work,' the Doctor interrupted. 'I just can't see how it *did*. This –' he gestured at Vincent's set-up – 'could have exploded a lemon, or made a frog's leg twitch, but there's no way it could have created

Frankenstein's monster. Running a current through dead matter doesn't bring it to life.'

'What about a defibrillator?' Rose asked. 'That can start a heart if it's stopped, right?'

'Nope. It can only synchronise the rhythm of heart muscles that are beating out of time, like the pat-a-cake rhyme in virtual reality.'

'What in Heaven's name are you talking about?' Vincent demanded. 'Criticise the particulars of my apparatus all you like, but the point is moot, because my experiment worked. The creature sat up.'

'Yes.' The Doctor touched a thoughtful finger to his nose. 'It did.'

Thunder crashed somewhere in the distance.

'It is out there,' Vincent said. 'While I am in here.' He sagged like a puppet on loose strings and lowered himself on to a stool. He looked at the Doctor and Rose, beaten. 'I am trapped. And now, I'm afraid, so are you.'

The Long Table

The Patchwork Man moved through the gardens with unnatural speed and grace, his hulking form slipping through hedgerows and over flower beds. His boots landed with barely a sound on the damp earth. Lightning flashed behind him, throwing his misshapen shadow forward. A storm was coming. He welcomed it. Usually, in weather like this, he would stand on a hilltop, gripping one of the lightning rods. Each blast from the sky made him stronger.

But right now, he had more than enough strength for his mission.

The front door was nearest to the gate, so it would be monitored the most closely. Therefore, he had followed the inside of the wall round to the back of the grounds so he could approach one of the manor's rear doors. It had taken a long time, but he was a creature of great patience.

They, however, were not. They were speaking to him in a chorus of sibilant whispers: *Thirsty*.

'Soon,' he murmured softly, though it was unlikely that anyone in the house would hear over the thunder.

Not soon, They said. *Now.*

He longed to fight them. Though his body was an abomination, he believed his mind retained a spark of humanity. Or did he only *want* to believe that? What was he, really? The more he asked himself this question, the further he felt from the answer.

'We agreed,' he growled.

We are thirsty. You will submit.

Their anger was rising, and with it, the pain. Hot and sharp, as though his spine were a spike and his brain balanced upon the point. Waves of nausea swept through his body, almost making him lose his footing. He steadied himself against the bough of a nearby apple tree. It vibrated, making the leaves shiver.

'One,' he gasped. 'I shall find you *one* victim.'

Soon, They said.

'Soon,' he agreed, and at last the pain receded.

He let go of the tree. He found himself gasping for air, even though since awakening on the scientist's workbench he'd found he could hold his breath indefinitely. He stood in the drizzle, feeling the pinpricks of cold against his grey skin. While They hated puddles, They didn't seem to mind rain.

Do not keep us waiting, They said. *Or we shall find another host.*

Rose followed Vincent and the Doctor down a wallpapered corridor with frayed skirting boards, illuminated by more low-watt bulbs.

'We've been under siege for some time now,' Vincent explained, 'so I'm afraid there are limits upon our hospitality.'

'No ketchup?' Rose guessed. 'Or cheese?'

'I'm . . . afraid not.' Vincent looked befuddled.

Rose shot an *I-knew-it* look at the Doctor, who simply shrugged. 'We're not fussed,' he said. 'It's kind of you to have us.'

Vincent pushed open a set of double doors with wrought-iron handles, revealing a large dining room with a long table, oak shining in the light of the candelabras. The table was big enough to seat twelve, but was set for four. One of the spots was taken by Vincent's father, who had cutlery clenched in both hands like a mad king. The others were empty.

'Aren't there six of us?' Rose said.

Vincent looked puzzled. 'I beg your pardon?'

Rose guessed the servants didn't eat with their masters, even while the house was under siege.

Frankenstein Senior confirmed this: 'Are you a simpleton? Who would bring us our food if the servants ate *with* us?'

Rose raised a brow. 'Interesting question, Mr –' she tried to remember the name of the rich jerk in *Pride and Prejudice*, and got there just in time – 'Collins.'

'Frankenstein,' the old man barked.

'Wrong book, Rose,' the Doctor whispered.

Rose didn't admit she'd only watched the miniseries. 'Sick burn, though, right?' she whispered back.

'Definitely. Very classy.'

Frankenstein Senior seemed to hear none of this. He was looking towards a narrow door at the far end of the room as though wondering where the servants – and his dinner – were. Rose took the seat furthest away from him.

'How did you meet Elspeth?' she asked Vincent as he took the seat opposite her.

'We are cousins,' Vincent said airily.

Rose's shock must have shown on her face because the Doctor nudged her. 'Nineteenth century,' he whispered.

'My aunt, Carol, adopted her on a trip to England,' Vincent went on. 'She was orphaned, you see. Carol has always been kind.'

'*Too* kind.' Frankenstein Senior was listening again. 'I'd never have allowed it if I'd known it would some day taint my bloodline.'

Rose's mouth fell open. 'You'd have preferred for Vincent to marry his *biological* cousin?'

'Exactly,' the old man said, turning to Vincent. 'See, boy? Even this bit of totty understands.'

'Excuse me?!' Rose demanded.

'Oi –' the Doctor began.

'*Father!*' Vincent shouted, and then lowered his voice. 'I'll not allow you to speak ill of my guests. Nor of Elspeth, who I love dearly. Is that understood?'

Frankenstein Senior looked faintly impressed with his son. Rose was, too. *Vincent has a spine after all*, she thought. *I hope he didn't steal it from a grave*.

'Apologies,' the old man grumbled.

Before Vincent could answer, the narrow door opened. Janine entered, carrying two heavily laden plates on one arm, like a waitress. Rose guiltily noted that Janine had had only an hour, at most, to read.

'Thank you,' Rose said, as Janine put a plate of roasted vegetables in front of her.

'Much obliged,' the Doctor said cheerfully. He hated injustice, but seemed better able than Rose to disguise his feelings. Rose wondered what he had been like as a young Time Lord, when he first started exploring the universe. Had he picked fights everywhere he went?

Janine said nothing as she returned to the kitchen.

'What happened to Elspeth's birth parents?' Rose asked.

'Elspeth's mother died in childbirth,' Vincent was saying, 'and her father of a broken heart. I didn't learn of this until years after the adoption. I was working on my scientific inquiries into the vital spark, hoping that some day my work could reverse all but the most violent of deaths.'

It seemed inappropriate during this little monologue, but Rose was very hungry. She took a bite of the sweet potato, which was divine.

'I had thought perhaps Elspeth's constitution would prove too delicate for such discussions,' Vincent went on, 'but when I revealed it to her, she was as impassioned as I. Of course, after she shared with me the fate of her parents, I understood.'

Rose nearly choked on the mouthful of vegetables. 'You want to bring her parents back?'

Vincent's eyes widened. 'No, no! Only to spare others the same fate. But our vision bonded us. Elspeth is the only person who understands my desires.' Vincent said this with a brief glare at his father, which seemed to go unnoticed.

As strange as it was to visit other centuries and be exposed to their prejudices, Rose found moments like this the most jarring – the moments when someone said something that felt totally familiar. Something like, 'My parents don't understand me, but my girlfriend does.'

'We'll protect her,' Rose promised.

The Doctor swallowed a mouthful of carrot. 'Of course we will,' he said. 'I already have step one of a plan.'

'Which is?' Rose asked.

'Get my sonic screwdriver back.'

The Transported Key

As they were about to go outside, Vincent patted his pockets and frowned. 'The key,' he murmured. 'I've lost it.'

'You dropped it,' Rose remembered. 'On the driveway.'

'I did?' Vincent was aghast. 'Thank God I locked the gate first. Why did no one tell me?'

Rose raised an eyebrow. 'I tried, but you were busy fleeing in terror.'

The Doctor looked pleased. 'Now we have step two of a plan! Things are progressing nicely.'

'What's step two?' Rose asked.

'Get my sonic screwdriver,' the Doctor said. 'And we have a new step one – find the key.'

'Only you could see that as "progress",' Rose said.

'Perhaps turning off the fence should be considered a separate step,' the Doctor mused. 'Then we would have three.'

'I'm not sure making the plan *longer* gets us closer to the end of it.'

'I fear the lady is right,' Vincent said, and Rose warmed

to him a little. She was usually right, but other people rarely admitted it. 'And I'm still unsure as to what kind of Doctor needs a screwdriver to do his work.'

'It's a *very* good screwdriver,' Rose said.

'It's sonic,' the Doctor explained.

Vincent looked baffled. 'I fear I am moving away from understanding rather than towards it.'

'You don't need to understand,' the Doctor said. 'Just trust us. We'll save Elspeth – and you! – before the big wedding.'

Vincent looked relieved, and then doubtful. 'How?'

'All in good time,' the Doctor said, which presumably meant he had no idea.

Vincent got to work unbarricading the door. 'We cannot stay out there for long,' he whispered as he worked. 'It is not safe.'

'No kidding,' Rose said.

'Don't fret.' The Doctor rubbed his hands together. 'We'll grab the key and go out of the gate. You switch off the negative energy field, I'll grab my sonic, and we'll be back inside in a flash.'

Right on cue, lightning lit up the windows. Thunder boomed a second later.

Rose had a bad feeling about this, but felt like she would be cursing them if she said so. She told herself that she and the Doctor had gotten out of worse scrapes.

Vincent pushed the doors open and they slipped through into the night.

It wasn't hard to follow Vincent's trail from a few hours earlier. The scuff marks and footprints had turned into muddy puddles. Soon, they arrived where Vincent had fallen and the Doctor had caught him by the braces.

There was no key.

'Are you quite certain that this is the spot?' Vincent whispered.

'Yes.' Rose pointed to where a copper coin glinted in the light from the windows, having flown out of Vincent's pocket when he fell. 'It must be here somewhere.'

The Doctor once again reached for his sonic and found the pocket empty. 'Bah,' he muttered.

They fanned out across the driveway, peering at the gravel, but the darkness made it hard to see much of anything. They hadn't brought lanterns, just in case the creature was nearby. They didn't want it to realise they were outside the house, exposed.

Rose was starting to think they needed a new plan – preferably one with a beginning, a middle and an end – when the Doctor whistled faintly. She looked over and saw him standing not far from the gate, holding up the key.

She jogged towards him, relieved. But something troubled her. Vincent had fallen back there, where the coins were. How had his key ended up all the way over here?

'Step one, sorted,' the Doctor whispered once Rose and Vincent had caught up to him. 'Where's the switch for the negative energy field?'

'Over there.' Vincent pointed to what looked like a small wooden crate. A long cable trailed from it to the wall.

'All right. Give us two minutes, then switch it off. Thirty seconds later, switch it back on.'

Vincent nodded and hurried away towards the box.

'Just you and me, Rose,' the Doctor said.

'You and me,' Rose agreed.

He quickly unlocked the gate, and they slipped through the gap.

Rose was surprised by how vulnerable she felt, outside the wall. She must have placed quite a lot of faith in Vincent's defences. She counted down from 120 in her head as they ran alongside the wall towards where they'd left the sonic screwdriver. The sooner they had it, the sooner they could get back inside.

This time, they ran in the right direction instead of taking the long way round. Rose was relieved to see the device still stuck to the wall. By her count, they still had a minute left.

'There she is!' the Doctor said. 'Step two is going well.'

Rose didn't want to celebrate just yet. 'How will we know when the fence is switched off?'

'The sonic will be released. And that humming noise will stop.'

Rose frowned and closed her eyes. The Doctor was right – the sound was loud and clear. Strange that she hadn't noticed it the first time they approached the wall.

In fact, the sound seemed to be coming from behind her.

Her eyes popped open and she whirled to face the trees –

Just as a figure lurched out of the forest.

The Missing Men

It wasn't the Patchwork Man. He was shorter and thinner. For a second, Rose was relieved – but then she saw the way he was shambling through the bush with both arms outstretched. She couldn't see his face in the dark, but a cold blue glow emanated from his eyes.

A second man emerged from the forest, a few metres further along the treeline. He was bigger and moved faster, but had the same stumbling gait. His head kept twitching as though flies were buzzing around it. Both men were dressed in battered riding clothes, like those worn by the people of Lamond, and were marching towards the front gate.

Rose grabbed the Doctor's arm. 'Who are they?'

She'd whispered the words, and the men were at least fifty metres away – but both their heads snapped round, the short one's neck twisting further than should be possible. Then, both men broke into a stumbling run towards Rose and the Doctor. As they approached, the ominous hum grew louder and louder. Soon, Rose could hear them muttering:

'Thirsty, thirsty, thirsty.'

'Doctor?' Rose cried. 'What's going on?'

'Nothing good.' The Doctor raised his voice: 'Let me guess: Haisman and Boucher?'

Neither man slowed down. It took Rose a moment to remember where she'd heard the names: from Bergam, at the Charging Ram. These were his friends, the ones who had gone into the forest and never returned.

They were shouting now. 'Thirsty! Thirsty!'

'Okay, Rose, here's the plan,' the Doctor said.

Rose was backing away from the men. 'It better not have too many steps!'

'In about twenty seconds, Vincent will switch off the negatively charged fence,' the Doctor said, 'and we're going to climb over the wall.'

Rose didn't take her eyes off the approaching figures. 'We don't have twenty seconds.'

'Yes, we do, assuming these blokes keep running at exactly the same speed, and that Vincent can count. We're going to climb fast, because we don't want to be touching the wire when he switches the fence back on. You don't have a spare heart to protect you. Ten seconds, now. Ready?'

The two shambling creatures had nearly reached them. Rose had never felt less ready in her life. 'And if they speed up, or if Vincent can't count, or something else goes wrong?'

'Then I suppose we'll find out what they want. Five seconds.'

'They've been very clear about what they want. They're thirsty.' Rose wished she still had that mug of metheglin. 'They want to *drink us*. Like that pig!'

There was a sudden shift in the air right behind her. The

fence hissed like water on an oily saucepan, and the sonic screwdriver fell off the wall.

The Doctor caught it before it touched the ground. 'Go!'

Rose would usually be reluctant to touch a fence that had been electrified – or negatively charged, or whatever – only moments ago. But the creatures with the glowing blue eyes were so close that she could see the drool on their chins, the veins popping on their foreheads and the dirt under the nails of their frantically grabbing hands. So she didn't hesitate. She threw herself at the wall, out of the men's reach.

The chicken wire wasn't designed for climbing. It cut deep into her fingertips as she pulled herself upward, but at least it didn't peel off the wall. Her hands fared better than her feet. Her boots scrabbled uselessly against the wire, unable to get a grip.

'Don't let them touch you,' the Doctor shouted, just as she felt a hand close round her boot.

Rose lashed out, slamming her heel into something hard. There was an awful crunch, and suddenly her foot was free. But when she attempted to continue the climb, she realised that her boot had slipped off. The chicken wire cut through her thin sock.

The Doctor had reached the top of the wall. 'Hurry!'

'I'm trying!' Rose bellowed. She scrambled up the wire towards him.

'Thirsty, thirsty,' snarled the creatures below.

The Doctor reached down with one hand, straddling the wall like it was a horse. Rose felt one of the creatures grab at her other boot, but she shook it off before it could get a solid grip. She launched herself upward, both arms outstretched, managing to grab the Doctor's hand. He pulled her up on to the top of the wall and hugged her.

'Hold on,' he shouted, and then pitched sideways. Rose screamed as the pair rolled off the top of the wall and plummeted towards one of Vincent's flower beds.

The Doctor hit the dirt first, and Rose landed on top of him, hard enough that she felt the air whoosh out of his lungs. She wriggled sideways, leaving him wheezing on the ground.

Rose tried to stand up, but the world was still spinning, and she collapsed on to the grass next to the flower bed. She found herself on her back, looking up at the night sky –

And the two creatures, who were clambering over the wall.

'Look out!' Rose yelled.

But suddenly there was another shift in the air, and the chicken wire crackled. The two creatures thrashed like ravers, and then went limp. Both of them fell off the wall and slammed into the ground, the short one still holding Elspeth's boot.

Rose scrambled away from them, heart pounding. Neither of them moved.

'Are they dead?' she demanded.

The Doctor sat up. He reached for his sonic screwdriver and then seemed to think better of it. He felt for a pulse on the tall man's throat instead.

'Yes.' He checked the other man. 'They've been dead for at least two days.'

'They were just chasing us.' She felt stupid saying this, but someone had to.

'No. Something inside them was chasing us, using their bodies for transportation. Whatever it was, the fence sucked it out of them.' The Doctor pulled Elspeth's boot out of the shorter man's hand and tossed it to Rose. She caught it and tugged it back on to her foot.

'I don't see any stitches,' she said. 'Is this another one of Vincent's experiments?'

The Doctor looked troubled. 'I don't think –'

A distant scream of terror split the night. They both looked up.

'That came from the house,' the Doctor said.

'Janine,' Rose breathed, and they both broke into a run.

The Conflicted Monster

They met Vincent halfway up the driveway. He, like them, was running towards the house.

'I only switched off the fence for thirty seconds,' he babbled. 'Could the monster have climbed over?'

'No,' the Doctor said, still sprinting. 'It was already here. It must have somehow gotten the key and let itself in through the main gate.' He dashed towards the house, Vincent right behind him. Rose brought up the rear, wading frantically through her petticoats.

Soon, they reached the manor. The Doctor wrenched the doors open, and they all tumbled inside.

They found the big coachman stumbling around the sitting room with a straight razor in one hand and shaving cream on his chin.

'I heard a scream,' he barked, glaring at Rose. 'Was it you?'

'No.' Rose looked around. 'Janine!' she yelled.

Vincent was shouting, too. 'Janine? Where are you?'

There was no answer.

'Split up. Find her.' The Doctor hurried up the grand staircase, taking the steps three at a time. Rose followed him, while Vincent and the coachman ran in separate directions to search the ground floor.

The Doctor turned right at the top of the stairs. Rose turned left. The first door she passed was only one metre square, set into the wall at waist-height with a crank mounted next to it. Just in case Janine was hiding inside the dumb waiter, Rose opened it, revealing a miniature lift shaft. Two thick ropes hung down to the floor below, where the box must be. There was no sign of the housekeeper.

She heard the Doctor say, 'Oh, hello!' from somewhere behind her. She thought maybe he'd found Janine, but then old Mr Frankenstein's outraged voice rang out: 'What the blazes are you doing in my bedroom? I've got a good mind to give you a thrashing . . .' The voice trailed off into a fit of coughing.

Leaving the Doctor to sort that out, Rose ran along the corridor, boots creaking on the hardwood floor, and knocked on the next door. 'Janine?' she called, her throat tight with fear as she turned the handle and pushed it open.

She found a small room – a woman's, she was sure. The furnishings were bare and practical. Pillows were neatly placed up one end of a narrow bed. The curtains billowed in the cold breeze from an open window. Approaching it cautiously, Rose peered out into the gloomy night. The moon cast a pale glow over the surrounding woods and gardens, but there was no movement.

'Janine!' she called, but was answered only by noises from outside, the hoot of an owl and the flapping of bat wings.

She went back into the corridor and checked the

bathroom. It was empty, the bathwater no longer steaming, all but one of the candles snuffed out. The mirror had fogged up. Before she turned away, Rose noticed an unusual pattern in the fog – stripes of thick and thin mist, like a barcode, or like . . .

An interference pattern. The words popped into her head in the voice of her Year Eight science teacher, but she couldn't quite remember the content of the lesson.

She reached out and touched the mirror. The glass felt cold, but not abnormally so. She wiped the fog away with her palm, revealing her reflection –

And that of a figure standing right behind her.

Rose almost leapt out of her skin. But it was just the Doctor.

'No sign of Janine down that end,' he said. 'Don't visit Mr Frankenstein Senior for a while – he's a bit cross, for some reason.'

'Wasn't planning on it,' Rose said. 'Let's go downstairs. Maybe the others have had more luck.'

'Maybe.' But the Doctor didn't meet her gaze as he said this. They both knew that Janine had screamed, and the fact that she now wasn't responding was a bad sign.

The grand old house was eerily quiet as they hurried back down the spiral staircase. Rose noticed for the first time the cobwebs draped over the chandelier and the statue of Prometheus. The Titan seemed to be watching her with sad eyes. And was it Rose's imagination, or were the electric lights buzzing at a different frequency? The flicker seemed more urgent, agitated – even excited. Something was going on here, something beyond the mere presence of Dr Frankenstein and his monster.

Vincent was at the bottom of the stairs, his face creased with worry. 'I can't find her anywhere,' he said.

'Nor me,' the coachman said, appearing from a hidden doorway beside the fireplace. This time, Rose got a glimpse of the dark, narrow passageway before the door swung closed and became once again part of the wall.

'Have you checked the stables?' Vincent asked.

'Aye. Naught there but the two mares.'

'Has either of you checked the kitchen?' Rose asked.

Blank looks all around.

'It's not suppertime,' Vincent said. 'Why would she be in there?'

Rose didn't wait for them to discuss it. She raced towards the kitchen.

The room had a low ceiling, made hazardous by ladles and tongs dangling from the beams. There was a potbelly stove dangerously close to the wooden cabinets.

The housekeeper stood in the centre of the room, facing away from them. Her back was straight and her hands were behind her, as if she were tied to an invisible post.

'Janine?' Rose said cautiously.

The housekeeper didn't move a muscle. The room was ice-cold, even though the stove was lit.

Rose approached cautiously. 'We thought we heard a scream,' she said. 'Are you okay?'

Janine still didn't turn round.

Rose circled around so she could see Janine's face. She had

been worried that the housekeeper would be dead somehow, even though she was upright. But Janine was alive, though very pale. She was staring, wide-eyed, at the closed door.

'Janine,' Rose said again, reaching out to touch the housekeeper's shoulder.

Janine's hand shot out from behind her back and grabbed Rose's wrist, crushing her tendons.

'Ow!' Rose cried.

'He said he wouldn't let them hurt me,' Janine whispered. 'No matter what.' Tears filled her eyes. Her claw squeezed Rose even tighter.

'Who?' Rose asked urgently.

'He said they could have the others,' Janine continued. 'But not me.'

The Doctor appeared by Rose's side. He held up a jelly baby. 'Take this,' he told Janine.

After a moment, the housekeeper let go of Rose's wrist. 'What's that?'

'A sweet.'

Janine put it in her mouth and chewed thoughtfully.

'It's good, isn't it?' the Doctor said.

Janine kept chewing.

'She's in shock,' the Doctor murmured. 'The sugar will help.'

Vincent rested a hand on Janine's shoulder. 'I'm so glad you're all right,' he said. 'I don't know what I'd do if I lost you.'

As Vincent comforted Janine, the Doctor and Rose backed away for a private conversation near the warmth of the stove.

'So what are we thinking?' Rose whispered. 'The monster comes in, threatens to hurt Janine, decides not to, and then leaves again?'

'Doesn't add up, does it?' the Doctor said.

Vincent draped a tea towel over Janine's shoulders, like a short scarf. 'Tell me what happened,' he said.

A little of the colour had returned to Janine's cheeks. 'I was reading, milord.' She pointed to a leather-bound book that had fallen on the floor. Predictably, it was *Frankenstein*. 'And there was a knock at the door. A voice said, "It's me." I looked through the little window and saw someone – but he'd turned away, and in the dark I thought he was the coachman.'

A memory hit Rose. When she was a kid, she and Shareen used to play a game where they would phone a random number, say 'It's me', and then see how long they could keep the conversation going before the person at the other end of the line realised they were talking to a stranger. Rose's record was forty-five seconds. It felt a bit like karma that the monster had entered the house using the same ruse.

'I shouldn't have unlocked the door,' Janine was saying, 'but I did, and then I saw his face. That horrible, hideous face! Like a nightmare come to life!'

Vincent's own face was filled with horror, and something else. Guilt. It was his creation she was describing.

'I screamed, and he reached for me.' Janine made her hands into clamp-like shapes. 'As if preparing to wring a chicken's neck. But then he started . . . I don't know, milord. Twitching. Like his clothes were full of bed bugs.'

'And he said he wouldn't let *them* hurt you?' Rose said.

Janine nodded. 'I didn't understand.'

Nor did Rose. But she remembered what the monster had said in the graveyard: *I keep Them fed in exchange for autonomy.*

'Father,' Vincent said suddenly. 'I must warn him.' He turned to run back towards the stairs. Then there was a pop, and all the lights went out.

The Headless Statue

Travelling with the Doctor, Rose had learned that space wasn't actually that dark. It surprised her every time, the way being outside the Earth's atmosphere clarified everything, turning the sky into a rich velvet, strewn with millions of sparkling diamonds. It was possible to sit in the open doorway of the TARDIS as it floated through the void and read a book by starlight alone.

But midnight in the nineteenth century, in a house with a monster after the power had just gone out – *that* was dark. Rose opened her eyes wider and wider until it hurt, but she still couldn't even see her own feet.

'Doctor,' she whispered.

'I'm here,' he said from somewhere to her right.

She reached for his hand and found it. A moment later, his sonic buzzed, and the kitchen filled with the familiar blue glow. Rose was very glad they'd gone back to retrieve it. Otherwise, they'd be fumbling around in the dark, searching for candles.

Rose quickly let go of his hand, a little embarrassed. 'I was worried the negative energy had killed it,' she whispered.

'No.' The Doctor tapped the side of the sonic. 'It has a failsafe. If anything tries to drain it, the whole thing locks down, trapping the charge inside.'

Rose was about to ask another question when she noticed something. There had been five people in the room when the lights went out. Now, only four remained.

She looked around. 'Where's Vincent?'

'Dr Frankenstein?' Janine called.

For a moment, there was no response – then a tremendous crash echoed through the house. And then a scraping sound, like claws against the inside of a coffin.

'Stay close to me,' the Doctor said. Rather than going to the exit, he headed for the sitting room. Moving *towards* the danger, as usual.

'I don't like this,' grumbled the coachman.

'That just means you're still sane,' Rose said.

As they crept through the sitting room, every shadow looked menacing. Even for such a large creature, there seemed to be endless hiding places. Standing inside the thick velvet curtains. Crouched behind the chaise-longue. Lurking around every doorway.

A voice filtered down from upstairs: 'Father?'

It was Vincent. When the lights went out, he must have persisted in his mission to find his dad. He knew the house well enough to move around in the dark.

'We need to talk to the creature,' the Doctor said. 'Give it a chance to . . .'

He trailed off as they entered the foyer. In the cold light of the sonic, Rose saw that the statue of Prometheus had been beheaded, and the chandelier wrenched off its chain, crystals scattered everywhere. One of them had been used to gouge a message in the wall:

> *YOU*
> *WILL*
> *DIE*
> *ALONE*

'I don't think talking can fix this,' Rose hissed.

'Father!' Vincent shouted from upstairs. 'Where are you?'

The Doctor hurried up the stairs, and Rose followed. 'It didn't hurt the housekeeper,' he said. 'In her description, the creature sounded conflicted. Don't you think?'

'It sounded *crazy*. Can we, you know, trap it somehow?'

They turned right, towards Frankenstein Senior's bedroom. The door was open. Rose could hear Vincent rummaging around in the darkness beyond.

Rose turned to the coachman. 'Are there enough horses for all of us?'

'There's a carriage,' he grunted. 'Room for six.'

As they entered the old man's room, the lights all came back on at once –

And Rose saw they would only need space for five.

The Shrinking Man

It was a grand bedroom with a sturdy wardrobe and a four-poster bed. A pair of leather gloves was neatly stacked on a bedside table. The electric light bulb fizzing overhead looked out of place, as did the ceramic light switch on the wall.

At first, the thing on the floorboards looked like a ventriloquist's dummy, dressed in clothes much too large. But those bushy brows were unmistakable. It was Vincent's father.

Vincent fell to his knees. 'No! Papa!' He took his father's wizened hand, but it crumbled like ash.

'What . . . how . . .?' Rose covered her mouth in shock and turned away from the scene. She felt like she might be sick.

'Explosive dehydration.' The Doctor crouched over the body. 'A human body is mostly water. If it all evaporates at once, the remains are significantly smaller, as you can see.'

Rose had seen this before with the pig, but she was no closer to understanding it. 'How is the creature doing this?'

'It doesn't make sense,' the Doctor muttered. 'Vincent,

was this what happened to your laboratory technician when the creature touched him?'

Vincent didn't seem to hear. He was sobbing, his hands clutching at the empty air like he could catch his father's escaping soul.

Rose ran to the curtains and pulled them aside. She had an irrational hope that the creature would have fled after killing Frankenstein Senior. But no, the window was closed and barred. The thing hadn't gone out that way.

'I heard a sound.' Janine was in the doorway. 'A sort of... pop. Like a gunshot.'

The Doctor's eyes narrowed. 'Or perhaps like a fuse blowing.'

Rose wasn't sure how a blown fuse could account for the disappearance of all the water in an old man's body. She grabbed the housekeeper's arm. 'Is there a room with a strong door? One that can be locked and barricaded?'

'The b-basement,' Janine stammered. 'Dr Frankenstein keeps unused equipment down there. Why?'

Vincent was gently lowering his father on to the bed. The Doctor grabbed him by the collar and hauled him away.

'But I can save him,' Vincent cried. 'I can bring him back!'

Rose had seen many miracles. But she didn't think any amount of electricity on Earth could resuscitate a man who had shrunk to the size of a dummy.

'I'm sorry,' the Doctor said. 'He's gone.'

Vincent moaned as they pulled him out of the door.

The Crown of Cups

The basement had a grooved floor, perhaps for drainage in the event of a flood. Sacks of flour and jars of preserves lined wooden shelves. As Janine lit a candle, Rose helped Vincent drag an old steamer trunk in front of the door.

'Will that hold?' Janine asked.

Rose thought of the sheer size of the creature pursuing them. 'I think so,' she lied.

Vincent sat on a barrel in the corner, weeping.

The Doctor was studying a stack of metal discs in the corner – they looked to Rose like weights from a home gym set-up.

'A voltaic pile,' he said thoughtfully. 'And here –' he examined a tray filled with glasses of brine, wires stretching from one to another – 'a crown of cups. This is how you were storing the lightning?'

Vincent looked at him with haunted eyes. 'What does that matter now?'

The Doctor swept his sonic screwdriver over the tray. It whirred. He frowned, studying the read-out. 'There's still electricity here.'

Vincent shrugged morosely. 'I assume the creature awoke before the entire charge was expended.'

'But the energy is *structured*. It's . . .' The Doctor pulled a yellow party balloon out of his pocket and put it to his lips. The others watched in bafflement and alarm as he inflated it.

'What in heaven's name are you doing?' Vincent asked.

Rose held up a calming hand. 'Just give him a minute.'

The Doctor tied a knot in the balloon and started waving it around. 'Static electricity,' he muttered. 'But it's *radiant*. How? It doesn't make any sense. Unless . . . oh no.' His eyes widened, and he backed away from the tray as though it were radioactive. 'We're not safe in here. Nobody touch the tray. Nobody touch *anything*. This house is infested with them.'

'Infested with *what*?' Rose demanded.

The Doctor didn't seem to hear her. He was pacing around the room. 'That's why the monster came to life, even though the experiment was set up wrong. It's not the monster, it's the things *inside* it, a billion subatomic puppeteers –'

Rose grabbed his arm. 'Doctor. What are you talking about?'

'Voltigrades,' the Doctor said ominously, and even though Rose had never heard the word before, the hairs on the back of her neck prickled.

'What are they when they're at home?' she asked.

'Living electricity.' The Doctor whirled round and pointed a finger at Vincent. 'Your father wasn't killed by your creation. He died because he touched the light switch.'

Vincent boggled at him. 'You're saying he was electrocuted?'

'No. He was *consumed*. By creatures living in the wires.

They feed off electrolytes, you see. Usually, it's just a drop of water here or a molecule of salt there – you'd hardly notice. But when enough Voltigrades form a group, they can devour all the moisture in your body like *that*.' He snapped his fingers, and Rose noticed how much it sounded like a fuse blowing. 'Or, if you seem like a good host, they might turn you into a puppet. You'd still die, but they could keep you moving around for weeks afterwards, looking for a juicier morsel.'

'How can electricity be alive?' Rose asked.

The Doctor huffed impatiently. 'You humans have a very narrow definition of life. As far as you're concerned, if it doesn't have DNA, it's not alive. You don't think the TARDIS is alive even though she feels. Even though she brought us here to help *you*.' The Doctor whirled round to face Vincent.

'Who is the TARDIS?' Vincent asked.

'The point is that life on this planet began when some atoms formed molecules, the molecules formed cells, and the cells started copying themselves and forming complex structures. Well, guess what? You don't need DNA to pull that off. You don't even need whole atoms. If electrons are arranged in the right way, they can form structures that grow, and eat, and multiply – which, in my view, is a much better definition of life.'

Vincent looked like he was struggling to keep up. 'You are hypothesising a sort of organism made of electricity?'

'Hypothesising? No. These creatures exist.'

'Like some kind of electric alien ... bacteria?' Rose suggested.

'Nothing alien about them. They form naturally in cumulonimbus clouds, right here on Earth, though humans don't discover them until 2063. Voltigrades are rare enough that there's usually a trillion-to-one chance of them meeting up and forming structures large enough to think and plan. Unless some idiot –' the Doctor turned to Vincent – 'spent months funnelling lightning from all over the countryside *into a single battery*.'

'Idiot?' Vincent spluttered. 'I have a doctorate from Cambridge!'

'Good for you. If they award professorships posthumously, I expect you'll be eligible *very* soon. Because these things are more powerful, literally, than you can imagine.'

Rose looked towards Janine and the coachman, but neither seemed willing to join the conversation. The coachman was clutching his whip and scanning the room as though a horse might be hiding among the shelves, while Janine still looked like she was in shock.

Rose wasn't far behind. Being hunted by Frankenstein's monster had been bad enough, but the thought that the creature was actually possessed by intelligent electricity was a lot to take in. 'How can they think if they're too small to have brains?' she asked.

'A lone Voltigrade can't think. An individual neuron can't, either,' the Doctor said. 'But eighty billion neurons all clustered together, sending little zaps back and forth – *that* can think. Unfortunately, it often doesn't.' He glared at Vincent. 'Do you understand what you've done?'

Vincent blinked helplessly. 'Less and less, it seems.'

'It took nearly four billion years for single-celled organisms to evolve into structures as complex as humans. You forced the process to happen instantly, creating a form of life unlike anything that has ever existed on this planet before.' The Doctor loomed over Vincent, his voice thick with quiet fury. 'And do you know what happens to an ecosystem when you introduce a brand-new apex predator?'

Vincent's expression was blank. Terms like 'ecosystem' probably didn't exist yet. But Rose understood the Doctor's meaning.

'You're saying this thing could multiply?' she said.

'I'm saying if we got in the TARDIS right now and went to your time, there might be no humans left. No other animals, either. At least, not the kind you'd recognise. It could be a whole new biosphere, filled with electrical creatures instead of organic ones. It's happened on other planets, and it could easily happen here.'

'Other planets?' Vincent echoed.

'I don't have time to open your mind for you,' the Doctor snapped. 'But here's a good starting point: humans are not above nature. You are part of it – just one of over five billion species that have evolved on this planet alone. More than ninety-nine per cent of those species are already extinct. Reflect on that.' He turned to Rose and lowered his voice. 'All right, we're in trouble.'

'I got that, thanks. These Voltigrades – how do we get rid of them? Is there some kind of, I dunno, electrical antibiotic we can use? Can we fumigate the house with negative energy?'

The Doctor's expression was grim. 'We can't kill them.'

Rose hadn't really thought of it as killing. 'But they're just . . . particles. Little dots.'

'We *literally* can't,' the Doctor said. 'Energy cannot be created or destroyed – ask Einstein. The Voltigrades can't be killed.'

Rose opened her mouth, but no more words came. If even the Doctor thought it was impossible, then where did that leave them?

Then she saw a cheeky smile spreading across his face. 'They can, however,' he said, 'be trapped.'

The Iron Trap

The Doctor needed several items to build his Voltigrade trap, and unfortunately, most of them hadn't yet been invented. Rubber gloves? No. Bipolar transistors? No.

'Lithium-iron batteries? Not *ion*, mind you. *Iron*.' The Doctor exaggerated the R.

'I once hypothesised such a contraption,' Vincent said, 'but I worried it would not be safe.'

'Ironic,' the Doctor muttered, exaggerating the R again. 'All right, what about a plasma ray emitter? Don't look at me like that,' he said to Rose. 'Most technologies are older than you think. Pythagoras once let me borrow his pocket calculator. So, plasma emitter?' He turned hopefully to Vincent.

Vincent stared blankly back.

'No matter. Say, *that's* iron . . .' The Doctor swept his sonic screwdriver around a bracket holding up a shelf. 'Excellent.' He picked up a spool of copper wire from the dust. 'With Dr Frankenstein's help, I think I can use this to make a fairly powerful electromagnet.'

'I shall be of little use,' Vincent said. 'Thus far, my efforts have only made things worse.'

'Oi! None of that,' the Doctor said. 'If you want to be all gloomy, do it after we've saved the world.' He started unwinding the wire from the spool. 'We'll also need to create a Faraday cage. No point hoovering up the Voltigrades if they can scuttle right back out. I'll need leather gloves, a glass jar – oh, and salt. Enough to kill a Fendahleen.' His brow furrowed. 'Actually, that's not much salt at all. Enough to kill *ten* Fendahleen. Or –'

'We'll get you plenty of salt,' Rose promised, choosing not to question him further on what a Fendahleen was. 'What else?'

The coachman spoke for the first time since they'd entered the room. 'Forget salt. I'll get the rifle.'

'No guns,' the Doctor said sharply.

'I never met anything a properly placed lead ball wouldn't kill.'

'If you shoot the creature, you'll make it angry at best. At worst, you'll dissipate the cloud of Voltigrades, and anything nearby will be consumed. Understood?'

The coachman's eyes narrowed, but he said nothing.

Rose noticed the eerie humming sound again. Her heels tingled, and the hairs on her arms stood on end. She felt the overwhelming urge to *get out*. But was the thought her own, or were the creatures somehow talking to her?

'Doctor,' she said. 'If the Voltigrades eat moisture, why did the puddle hurt it?'

'Well, because . . .' The Doctor frowned. 'Actually, that's an excellent question. A deep puddle of dirty water would have far more electrolytes than a human being. Hang on.' He pressed his forefingers to his temples. 'That must have been the problem. The sheer volume of minerals in the water would have drawn some of the Voltigrades out . . .'

Rose nodded slowly. 'And then they would have been stuck there.'

'Exactly. A puddle is a less useful host than a person. Can't go anywhere, can't eat anybody. Or drink anybody, rather.'

'Could we fill the house with puddles, then? If the Patchwork Man steps in one, he'll lose some of his, I dunno, power?'

'He might,' the Doctor agreed. 'And then the next person to make contact with the water — probably one of us — would either be consumed by the Voltigrades or become their next host, depending on how hungry they are.'

'Oh.' Rose's cheeks grew hot. 'Well, that's that, then.'

The Doctor turned to the others. 'Right. I need as much salt, copper and iron as you can find. We'll have to split up while we search.'

'Hang about!' Rose held up both hands. 'I've seen horror films. That's a *terrible* idea.'

'Sorry, Rose. The closer we are to each other, the more the Voltigrades will be drawn to us. We're bunched together like a *very* high-calorie snack at the moment.'

Rose felt a shiver crawl up her spine. 'But what if the monster is still in the house?'

She hadn't heard anything for some time. But for all she knew, it could be waiting right outside the door.

'I'll stay within earshot.' The Doctor gestured to his large ears. 'If you see it, just yell for me. I have a few tricks up my sleeve.' He peered into the cuff of his coat as though checking that his 'tricks' were still there.

'You should all leave,' Vincent said quietly.

Everyone in the room turned to look at him.

'I did this,' he continued. 'I should be the one to undo it.'

The Doctor softened. He rested a hand on Vincent's shoulder as though he could pass down his centuries of experience.

'You'll get your chance to make this right,' he said. 'I promise.'

The Dusty Table

Janine headed for the kitchen, looking for salt. The coachman left the house to search for iron tools in the shed. Vincent and the Doctor stayed in the basement, Vincent unspooling the copper wire while the Doctor used his sonic screwdriver like a . . . well, like a screwdriver, for once. One by one, the screws fell out of the crumbling wall.

Rose hesitated in the basement doorway. 'Good luck,' she whispered.

The Doctor didn't look up from his work. 'Remember,' he grunted as he wrenched the iron bracket off the wall. 'Don't touch the light switches.'

'Not a problem,' Rose muttered to herself. She didn't want to touch *anything* in this spooky old house.

She'd seen a pair of leather gloves in the old man's room, so she made her way to the grand staircase. It was tempting to run up them – the sooner she had the gloves, the sooner she could rejoin the others – but she didn't want to make too much noise. The soft pattering of rain outside barely covered the creaking of the floor.

At the top of the stairs, she turned right, her eyelids

stretched wide against the dark. When she reached the bedroom, she nudged the door open with her elbow, wincing as it creaked.

Lightning flashed between the heavy velvet curtains, illuminating the four-poster bed, the slightly crooked wardrobe, and a hat rack with a big cloak draped over it. Thunder crashed. Rose crept towards the bedside table, where she'd noticed the gloves earlier. She tried to tiptoe, but Elspeth's boots made it difficult.

She reached out, feeling around the tabletop.

Just dust. The gloves were gone.

Frowning, she ran her hands across the smooth wood, checking that the table really was bare. Had the gloves been knocked down in the chaos when they'd discovered the body?

The body. It was presumably still on the floor, though the darkness was too thick to make it out. Rose shuddered and crouched down, checking around the table legs. No gloves.

She stood up, wiping her dusty hands on Elspeth's dress as she scanned the room. Finally, she spotted the gloves on the hat rack, poking out from under the cloak. She didn't recall seeing anyone put them there. Actually, she didn't remember noticing the hat rack at all.

It didn't matter. She'd found the gloves: that was what mattered. Relieved, she approached the rack and reached for them —

Just as the lightning flashed again, she saw that there was no hat rack.

Instead, a big man stood inside the cloak.

The gloves came to life, one grabbing her wrist and another clamping over her mouth. Two blue lights appeared before her.

'Hello, Elspeth,' the monster said.

The Face of Evil

Rose had never seen Vincent's monster close up. Now, in her terror, she could see little else. The room seemed to disappear, leaving only his wide jaw, teeth – all of which seemed to be molars – and his glowing eyes. A line of ragged stitches ran diagonally across his face. His breath was cold and smelled like her local butcher's shop.

'Do not struggle,' he said. His accent was formal, but his voice itself remained garbled, as though his tongue was too long for his mouth.

Rose ignored him, trying to squirm free. The Doctor had promised to stay within earshot. If she could just scream –

The creature squeezed her face and wrist even tighter. His strength was tremendous.

'*They* are hungry,' he said. 'If you touch my skin, They will consume you. And you have not yet served your purpose.'

His words penetrated the fog of panic, and Rose held still. She tried to talk, but the thick glove muffled her voice. She could hardly breathe.

Unexpectedly, the creature released her. 'Scream for your betrothed,' he commanded.

Rose opened her mouth to cry out for the Doctor, but stopped herself just in time. The monster *wanted* her to scream. She wasn't going to give in so easily.

'What do you want with – with Vincent?' she asked, trembling.

'Your beloved has wronged me,' the monster said coldly. 'I intend to wrong him in turn.'

She didn't tell him that Vincent wasn't actually her beloved. It didn't seem like a good idea to reveal that she had no value as a hostage.

'I saw your message downstairs,' Rose said. ' "You will die alone." You want me to summon Vincent because you want to kill me in front of him.'

The monster didn't deny this. 'Scream for me,' he said.

'No.' Rose wanted to sound defiant, but her voice wobbled, tears filling her eyes.

The monster's lip curled. 'You cannot arouse my pity. My visage inspires terror in everyone I meet. I am used to it.' He leaned forward, his glowing blue eyes fixed on hers. '*Scream.*'

Rose kept her mouth shut resolutely.

The creature lashed out, smashing a gloved fist into the wardrobe. The oak crumbled under the force.

'Test me not, girl,' he snarled. 'I could tear you limb from limb. Scream before I make you.'

'Listen,' Rose said. 'There's a man downstairs called the Doctor. He cares for all living creatures.'

'Dr Frankenstein cares only for infamy,' the creature growled.

'Not him. A different Doctor. The others in this house

would gladly see you shot, but not *my* Doctor. Surrender now, and I'll make sure it's him who finds you, not them.'

The creature threw her across the room like a rag doll. Rose's back hit the wall hard enough to knock the air from her lungs. She flung both hands out, searching for a weapon, and found the jagged edge of the hole in the wardrobe. She wrenched out a long, thick shard of wood and brandished it at the creature.

'Stay back!' she shouted. 'I'm warning you!'

The looming monstrosity looked unfazed. He stomped towards her, his boots making the floorboards bounce, reaching for her with big hands. Rose darted aside and, at the same moment, jabbed the makeshift stake into his chest.

The creature looked down at the spike protruding from his torso.

Rose scrambled backwards, one hand over her mouth. She couldn't believe what she'd just done. Would the creature collapse? Crumble to dust?

To her relief – but also dismay – the Patchwork Man merely smirked with his misshapen mouth and wrenched the stake out. Rose wasn't even sure it had penetrated his thick woollen cloak.

'I am no vampire,' the creature said, flinging the wooden spike into a shadowy corner. 'And I tire of your games.'

Rose backed into the bedside table. She grabbed a candlestick holder and swung it with all her might. The heavy base connected with the creature's temple. The impact sent shock waves up her arm.

The creature didn't even seem to notice. He grabbed her by the throat and lifted her off her feet. 'Scream,' he ordered.

Rose couldn't have, even if she'd wanted to. She gurgled in his grip, white spots flaring across her vision. Her head seemed to be inflating like a balloon. Soon, she was floating up, up, towards the night sky, even though she was indoors . . .

'Put. Her. Down.'

Rose couldn't turn her head to see who was speaking, but she would have known that voice anywhere. Her Doctor, with even more steel in his tone than usual.

The monster whirled round, and Rose whirled with him. Her feet finally found the floor again, and the pressure round her throat eased slightly. She sucked in a lungful of cold, musty air.

As the colour returned to her vision, she saw the Doctor in the doorway, his mouth a hard line, his eyes blazing. He was holding the iron bracket, mummified in copper wire.

'Let her go,' he said.

Rose felt the creature's voice as a dark rumble behind her back. 'You must be the Doctor,' he sneered. 'The one who cares for all living things.'

'I try,' the Doctor said evenly. 'But you're testing my patience.'

'My quarrel is not with you. I want Frankenstein.' The creature paused, as if hearing voices, and then repeated, 'I want Frankenstein.'

'Vincent never intended for you to suffer,' the Doctor said. 'He created you in a state of madness. He said he felt possessed. Something I'd expect you to understand. Because this isn't you, is it? It's *Them*.'

The monster ground his teeth. It sounded like boulders tumbling down a hill.

'I can help you,' the Doctor added.

'*No one can help me!*' the creature roared, so loudly that Rose flinched in his grip. 'Tell Vincent his bride-to-be awaits.'

The Doctor's eyes widened almost imperceptibly. He glanced at Rose, who gave the slightest of nods. With her eyes, she tried to say, *Yes, I'm letting him think I'm Elspeth*.

As subtle as this exchange was, the creature seemed to notice it. 'You . . .' he began, and then his body shifted behind Rose, turning towards the portrait leaning against the wall. Rose couldn't see it in the dark, but she remembered what was in it. Vincent, holding hands with Elspeth. A beautiful, dark-haired woman who looked nothing like Rose.

Apparently, the creature had better night vision than she did.

'You are not Elspeth,' he growled. 'Where is she?'

The Doctor raised the bracket. 'Let Rose go. This is your last warning.'

'You think you can threaten me with *that*?' The creature gestured at the bracket and the wires. 'I am not so easily cowed.'

He sounded fearless, but Rose noted that he was still using her as a human shield.

The Doctor hesitated, then said, 'Very well.' He put the bracket down in the doorway, then kicked it into the corridor, out of sight behind the wall.

Rose wanted to scream, *What are you doing?* But then she

caught the determined look in the Doctor's eyes and saw the sonic screwdriver in his hand.

The creature saw it, too. 'What is that?'

'Sonic screwdriver,' said the Doctor, who was honest to a fault. He often lied his way *into* trouble, pretending to be a telegraph pole inspector or whatever, but rarely lied his way out of it.

The creature didn't ask what a sonic screwdriver was. 'Put it down.'

'Certainly.' The Doctor made eye contact with Rose. He slowly lowered the screwdriver towards the floor –

Then Rose wrenched herself sideways, out of the creature's grip –

Just as the Doctor pointed the screwdriver at the hidden bracket and flicked a switch.

Suddenly the Patchwork Man stumbled, the electromagnetism dragging him towards the bedroom wall – or rather, towards the bracket on the other side of it. The creature spun round, as though fighting a strong wind, his boots sliding across the floor. He moonwalked for a moment, stomping forward but sliding backwards. The closer to the wall he got, the faster he moved, until eventually his back slammed against the wall.

'Witchcraft!' he roared, trying to peel his body off the wallpaper.

'Run!' the Doctor yelled, but Rose was already sprinting towards the doorway. She collided with him in the corridor and grabbed his hand, then they both dashed towards the stairs.

While You Burn

'I was hoping the Voltigrades would be sucked out of him,' the Doctor puffed as they fled. 'But they're holding on tight. They must *really* like their host.'

Rose was already hurtling down the stairs. 'How long will he be stuck?'

'Electromagnetism is a trillion trillion trillion times stronger than gravity.' The Doctor glanced down at the sonic in his hand. 'But this thing doesn't have infinite power.'

'Could've fooled me – how long?'

'The effect will last –' the Doctor counted on his fingers – 'twenty-seven years, give or take.'

'What?!' Rose threw up her hands. 'Why are we running, then?'

Upstairs, a giant fist smashed through the wall and started clawing around for the bracket.

'*That's* why,' the Doctor said.

Rose realised what he meant. The creature was pinned to the wall, but he was strong enough to take the wall with him.

They raced into the foyer, nearly tripping over the worn rug in their haste. 'Vincent!' the Doctor shouted.

'Janine! Mr . . .' He nudged Rose. 'What's the coachman's name?'

'Dunno! Coachman!'

'A job title instead of a name? Absurd,' said the Doctor. He raised his voice. 'Mr Coachman! We have to go, now!'

Vincent and the coachman both emerged from the basement. Vincent was carrying a hatbox. 'What's all that noise?' he demanded.

'Your creation. He knows Elspeth isn't here.'

There were more smashing sounds from upstairs. Rose heard breaking glass along with the shriek of bending metal.

Vincent's already pale face turned white. 'He'll go after her. She won't stand a chance –'

'We'll get to her first,' the Doctor promised, running towards the kitchen. 'The creature can't outrun the horses.'

'I'll get the carriage.' The coachman dashed towards the front door and slipped outside.

When the others barged into the kitchen, Janine was there, holding a clinking leather bag. 'Lots of jars; lots of salt.'

Rose grabbed the Doctor. 'Will that do any good?' she asked. 'Without the bracket and the wire?'

She could see the answer in his eyes. 'We'll bring it just in case.'

Vincent wrenched open the door to the pantry. He grabbed a burlap sack of flour and hugged it to his chest.

'What are you doing?' Rose demanded.

Vincent ran towards the parlour. 'It took my assistant,' he muttered. 'It took my father. It will not take my bride!'

'Vincent,' the Doctor warned. 'Don't!'

'What's going on?' Rose asked.

The Doctor was chasing Vincent, but he called back over his shoulder: 'Nineteen eighty-one! Oxfordshire! Why do you think custard powder explodes? Corn starch!'

Vincent was already on his knees, tearing open the sack. He hurled a fistful of the fine white powder into the fireplace. The flames brightened, and a sudden rush of heat rolled out across the room, drying out Rose's eyeballs and burning the air out of her lungs.

'Do you hear me, demon?' Vincent screamed, scooping up more starch. 'You will not take her!'

The Doctor grabbed the back of his shirt and tried to pull him away from the fireplace, but he'd already thrown the second handful. This time, there was a dull boom, the hot air pushing them both backwards. The corner of the rug was already smoking, the floorboards were turning black, and the whole room was beginning to shimmer.

'We have to get out of here,' Rose gasped, smoke stinging her nose.

Vincent was incoherent now, screeching and sobbing. Rose and the Doctor dragged him out of the parlour and back into the kitchen. The wind howled, the hungry flames sucking air through the smashed exterior door. Rose slammed the kitchen door but doubted that would stop the fire from spreading.

'What have you done?!' Janine grabbed Vincent and shook him. 'You'll burn this place to cinders!'

'Come on!' The Doctor turned towards the exit. But just as he got to it, a huge piece of debris fell out of the sky and landed right outside the door with a tremendous crash. It looked like part of the wall from upstairs. Rose just had time to wonder why it had fallen when the Patchwork Man landed in a crouch just beyond it, presumably having leapt through the hole he'd created.

The creature stood, unhurried. His cloak was smoking. He shrugged it off, then tossed it on to the debris. From one pocket he produced what looked like a bottle of scotch – perhaps the one the coachman had lost. The creature clenched the cork between his teeth and ripped it out, then poured the alcohol on to the burning cloak. Soon the debris was ablaze.

'No!' Vincent cried.

The creature glanced up, his monstrous form shimmering in the heat of the blaze. A leer spread across his mutilated face. 'Dr Frankenstein,' he said. 'Have you doomed yourself to deny me the satisfaction of killing you?'

Vincent didn't plead for his own life. Instead, he cried, 'Don't hurt Elspeth. I beg you. She is innocent in all of this.'

'She is.' The monster walked closer, seeming not to feel the heat of the flames. Rose saw that the shelf bracket was still stuck to the side of his torso. 'You are powerless to save her,' he went on, 'and your sins have caused her demise. It is not *just*. It is not *fair*. Reflect upon that as you burn.'

'Listen to me.' The Doctor's stern voice seemed to carry over the roaring flames: 'This is your last chance.'

The monster gestured at the burning house with a big hand. 'I rather think it's yours.' He turned and walked away, soon disappearing into the soup of shadows and smoke.

The Broken Crank

Rose tried to run out of the door, but the heat pushed her back. The blazing debris would burn her to ashes if she tried to get out that way. The only other door led to the living room, which would be fully ablaze by now.

'We need a different exit,' she cried. The heat scorched her throat when she inhaled.

'The creature just made one,' the Doctor said. 'Smashed clean through the wall on the upper storey.'

'Yeah, but the fire is between us and the stairs,' Rose said. 'Any other ideas?'

'The dumb waiter!' Janine pointed frantically at the small, square doorway. A crank was mounted on the wall beside it, just like the one upstairs.

The Doctor pulled open the door, stuck his arm into the box and buzzed his sonic screwdriver. After a few clunks, two bolts fell out. Then the Doctor pulled the whole box out of the shaft and tossed it aside, leaving a vertical tunnel to the next floor.

'Rose,' he said. 'Can it be done?'

Rose climbed in. It had sounded plausible in the abstract,

but as soon as she squeezed her body through the narrow gap into the pitch-black tunnel, she realised how difficult it would be. There was no ladder. No handholds or footholds. Just hot, rough wood.

'Nothing to hang on to,' she called. She'd have to crawl up the vertical shaft, bracing her hands and knees against one side and her back against the other. Even as a nineteen-year-old former Jericho Street Junior School gymnast, it would be hard. For the others, it might be impossible.

'I think we need a better plan,' she shouted.

'All right. Got one,' the Doctor said. 'Hang on!'

'To what?!' Rose demanded, but then the answer hit her – literally. She bumped her head on a hook that hung from a thick rope. This must have been how the box was raised and lowered. The crank was connected to the rope, which would go over a pulley somewhere in the darkness at the top of the shaft. She grabbed the hook with both hands.

'Up we go!' shouted the Doctor. He pointed the sonic at the crank and pushed the button. The crank started spinning, and the rope went taut, pulling Rose upward. She held in a scream as she zoomed up through the shaft like a rocket towards the pulley at the top. Just as her hands were about to get sucked into the mechanism, she let go of the hook and thrust her arms forward. The little door at the top of the shaft popped open. She managed to grab the door-frame and haul herself up and out, tumbling into the corridor at the top of the stairs. The smoke stung her lungs and made her eyes water.

'Not so quick next time,' she called, coughing.

The Doctor's voice floated up the shaft, barely audible over the crackling flames. 'Might not have much choice!'

The heat upstairs was overwhelming. Wallpaper bubbled all around Rose. On the nearby portrait, Vincent and Elspeth's faces were melting on to their clothes. If the others didn't all get up the dumb-waiter shaft soon, this corridor would become just one more dead end.

A few seconds later, Janine whizzed up the shaft, clinging to the hook and shrieking. Rose grabbed her when she reached the top and helped her climb out of the little doorway.

'Where was your friend . . .' Janine puffed, '. . . when I was . . . filling the tub?'

'He's pretty incredible,' Rose said. 'But don't tell him I told you.' She stuck her head into the shaft. 'Oi! Ready for the next one!'

Vincent made all the grunting and spluttering noises you'd expect from a posh dandy forced to climb into a narrow, dark, dirty dumb-waiter shaft. 'I say, I don't think this is likely to *wooooooork*!' He wailed as the rope, motorised by the sonic, suddenly hauled him up the shaft.

There was a sharp *snap* from somewhere down below. Vincent's ascent stopped about a metre short of the door. He clung to the rope, pedalling the empty air.

Rose reached down. 'Grab my hand!'

Vincent didn't let go of the rope. 'I can't!'

Rose had had just about enough of Dr Frankenstein. She leaned into the dumb-waiter shaft, grabbed his wrist and heaved. As soon as his arm was out, Janine grabbed it, too.

Between them, they managed to haul Vincent out of the shaft and into the smoky air of the upstairs corridor. He lay on the carpet, wheezing.

'Is he okay?' the Doctor called from below.

'Never mind him! Get up here!'

'Don't wait for me. I'll meet you outside.'

Rose's breath hitched in her throat. She recognised that tone. It was his *I'm-sacrificing-myself-to-save-everyone-else* tone.

She stuck her head into the hole. At the bottom of the shaft, the Doctor was holding the crank he'd used to wind the pulley. It was in two pieces and no longer attached to the wall. 'The sonic must have been a bit much for it,' he said. 'Thought that might happen.'

That's why he made the rest of us go first, Rose realised. 'Are you fireproof or something?'

The Doctor forced a smile. 'We'll find out.'

'Hold on to the rope,' Rose shouted, grabbing the crank beside the upstairs door. She pushed with all her might but couldn't make it turn. Vincent joined her, his hands next to hers on the handle. But even their combined strength wasn't enough to lift the Doctor.

Rose stuck her head back into the shaft. 'You need to fix that crank!'

'I can't.'

'You can! You've fixed more complicated things than that!'

The Doctor gave her a sad smile. 'Sometimes the simplest problems are the hardest to solve.' He held up the two pieces, showing Rose the break. It was hard to imagine how they could repair it in the time they had. 'I'm sorry. You have to go.'

'Use the sonic,' she said desperately.

'It's not a welding torch, Rose.'

'Why not?' Rose demanded. 'It's just about everything else!' She wiped the sweat out of her eyes. The heat gave her an idea. 'Okay. Melt some jelly babies in the fire, use them to stick the handle together, and use the sonic to cure it. Harden it.'

The Doctor laughed with real warmth. 'Rose Tyler,' he said, 'you're fantastic. Don't ever forget that, all right?'

'Stop complimenting me and do it!'

'I would if I could, believe me. But it's impossible.'

'Everything you do is impossible!'

There was a mighty *crack* from beneath her feet. The floorboards sagged in the middle, no longer supported by the beam below. For a terrifying moment, she thought she was going to fall right through the floor into the roaring flames. But the bending boards held her weight, for now.

She stuck her head into the shaft again. The walls had partly collapsed, leaving behind an unclimbable mess of wooden spikes. The rope was on fire now, strands blackening as they unwound. Soon, it would burn right through.

'I'm not leaving you,' she said.

'You have the key to the TARDIS,' the Doctor said. 'Once you're inside, just disable the entanglement drive and pump the tachyon bank. She'll understand what's happened. She'll take you home. Give my love to Jackie. Tell her I'm sorry.'

'Tell her yourself,' Rose snapped and grabbed the handle again. Maybe the Doctor was willing to accept his own death. But she refused. She would save him. Or die trying.

She pushed with all her might. Her muscles burned. Her tendons stretched to their limits. Her heart pounded, and her head throbbed. Slowly but surely, the crank made half a turn – and then her muscles gave out, and it fell back into position.

'Stand back,' Janine commanded.

Rose was too weak even to obey. It didn't matter. The housekeeper pushed her aside like she weighed nothing, grabbing the crank with both hands.

'Hold on, Mr Doctor,' she called, and started winding.

Rose watched with amazement as Janine toiled, sweat pouring down her face as the crank went round and round.

'Just like collecting water for a bath,' she grunted as she worked. 'He's barely four buckets' worth.'

Rose staggered to her feet in time to see the top of the Doctor's head appear in the open doorway –

And then the burning rope finally snapped.

Rose lunged for the Doctor just as he started to fall. She grabbed for his hand but got the sleeve of his coat instead. His weight pulled her halfway into the shaft, lifting her feet off the ground.

'Help me!' she shouted, but Vincent was already grabbing her legs, and Janine had gripped the Doctor's other arm. They pulled him up through the doorway, and then all four of them collapsed in a heap.

Vincent quickly let go of Rose's legs and scrambled to his feet. 'Forgive me,' he stammered. 'Of course, under usual circumstances I would not touch a lady in such a way –'

'Stop blabbering and run!' Rose shouted.

The Tornado of Flame

They sprinted along the corridor, sparks raining down on their heads, burning scraps of wallpaper waltzing through the smoke around them. Rose could barely breathe. She thought how tragic it would be if they made it this far only to suffocate.

But the air became clearer as they turned the corner and saw what the monster had done. It had smashed a hole clean through the wall, in roughly its own shape, like Rose had seen in old cartoons. Fresh, sweet air flowed through the gap, feeding the hungry flames behind them.

As Rose approached the edge, she heard the clip-clopping of hooves and the grinding of carriage wheels on muddy gravel. She stuck her head out into the pelting rain and saw the carriage approaching, horses pawing anxiously at the ground. She'd forgotten all about the coachman, who had gone to the stables before the fire started. He appeared to be shielding his face from the heat with a horse blanket.

The pile of burning debris was directly below Rose. The monster had simply leapt over it and landed in a superhero pose, but Rose figured she'd break both legs if she tried that.

Vincent leaned over her shoulder. 'The rain may extinguish the flames,' he said hopefully.

'Not in time,' Rose said. 'We need –' a storm of coughs rushed up her throat, but she choked them back down – 'a mattress. To land on.'

Janine looked back down the burning corridor. 'There's mattresses, milady, but I don't think we can get to them.'

'What a lot of hot air,' the Doctor said.

Rose shot him a glare, but he was busy looking down at the burning debris.

'Hot air,' he said again. 'Don't you see?'

He pointed his sonic down at the fire. The device whirred, the blue light glowing. Down below, the flames grew bigger and brighter.

Rose had to shout to be heard over the crackling blaze. 'Doctor! You're making it hotter!'

'That's the idea.' The Doctor kept the sonic trained on the fire. It kept growing, but it also changed shape, becoming a swirling tornado. The Doctor seemed to be charming it, like a piper with a snake. Soon, Rose could feel the scorching wind tugging at her hair.

'Are you mad?!' Vincent demanded.

The Doctor grinned. 'Yeah! Did I not mention that?'

The floor of the corridor creaked beneath them. The whole house could collapse at any moment.

'Doctor?' Rose said.

The Doctor kept his device trained on the flames below. 'The sonic,' he explained, 'is *sonic*.'

'Meaning what?!'

'Meaning sound waves, which means air pressure, which means I can funnel all the hot air into a single rotating column.'

'But why?' Rose asked, dreading the answer.

'Because hot air –' the Doctor pocketed the sonic and backed away from the hole in the wall – 'rises!'

The Doctor took a run-up and then leapt through the hole. He should have fallen right into the bonfire below. But to Rose's amazement, he sailed right over it, his clothes billowing, and landed on the roof of the parked carriage.

He turned to face them without even acknowledging the startled driver. 'Jump!' he shouted.

Janine and Vincent looked terrified.

'Well, don't hang about,' Rose said, sounding braver than she felt. She backed up into the scorching heat of the corridor, then took a run-up towards the hole, just as the Doctor had done. Every instinct screamed at her to stop.

Trust the Doctor, she told herself. She shut her eyes as she took the last three steps and jumped.

Immediately, she started to fall. For a moment she thought she'd made a terrible mistake. But then the wall of hot air hit her like a truck, catapulting her back into the sky. She screamed, the air burning right out of her lungs as she sailed over the flames, less like a hawk and more like a rubbish bag in a gale –

And then she slammed into the Doctor, his long arms round her, his leather coat in her face.

'It's all right; I've got you,' he said, as her feet found the roof of the carriage.

She scrambled gratefully down the side of the carriage to make room for the next person. The horses still looked uneasy, licking their floppy lips, eyes wide behind tattered blinkers. Rose patted the muscular flank of the closest one, hoping to calm it down. If it bolted, there would be no carriage for Janine and Vincent to land on.

'Have you got a carrot or something?' she shouted, but the coachman didn't respond. Rose could barely see him through the rain and smoke and shadow.

Vincent flew out through the hole in the wall, screaming, eyes squeezed shut. Like Rose, he started to fall, before floating over the flames into the Doctor's arms. The Doctor patted him on the back reassuringly, but Vincent didn't let go, sobbing with terror. Eventually, the Doctor peeled Vincent's hands off his leather coat and gave him a gentle nudge towards the edge. Rose helped Vincent climb shakily down the side of the carriage. He rested on all fours for a moment, unwilling to let go of the ground.

As silly as he looked, Rose sympathised. After bobbing through the air like that, she had the unsettling feeling that it might happen again – that she might just float away, like someone had forgotten to pay the gravity bill. Travelling with the Doctor was often like that. All the laws about how the world worked suddenly seemed unreliable, the ground never quite solid beneath her feet.

As Vincent recovered and climbed into the carriage, Janine hurtled overhead, her apron flapping wildly. She crashed into the Doctor with more force than Rose or Vincent had, and they both toppled off the far side of the carriage. But before Rose could even call out, they both emerged. Janine's face was white with terror, but the Doctor was beaming.

As Janine climbed in through the door, the carriage started to roll away. Maybe the coachman was sick of waiting. The Doctor stood on the running board, one hand outstretched for Rose.

She grabbed it and jumped. He pulled her through the open door, and they both landed on the velvet upholstery inside. Janine pulled the door shut, sealing out the rain and the roaring flames.

Rose pulled the lacy curtain back and watched through the window as the manor crumbled, glass breaking, iron bending, wood blazing, slates tumbling inwards. Finally, the roof collapsed under a column of black smoke, which corkscrewed up to join the storm clouds above.

The Treacherous Road

The opulent, relaxing interior of the carriage was jarring after their frenzied escape. Rose sank into a plush velvet seat next to Janine. The Doctor and Vincent sat opposite them, their knees bumping against a battered steamer trunk. Rose hoped there was food inside – it felt like years since she'd eaten – but it didn't seem appropriate to start rummaging yet, not when Vincent and Janine had just seen their home go up in flames.

Vincent pounded on the ceiling with one fist. 'Take us to the château at Loch Lamond!' he shouted. 'We need to rescue Elspeth!'

The coachman didn't reply, but Rose heard him flick the reins, urging the horses onwards through the stormy night. Rain lashed at the windows, thunder rumbling as the burning manor shrank into the distance.

'What will happen to the Voltigrades in the house?' Rose asked. 'The ones living in the wires?'

The Doctor shrugged. 'They'll disperse as the house breaks apart. Instead of one big structure, like a person, they'll become a million little structures, like bacteria. Too small to have consciousness.'

'Could they group together again, though?'

'Doubt it. Remember, they didn't come together naturally in the first place – they were *forced* together, by someone who should have known better.' He glanced at Victor. 'Burning down your own house was a stupid idea – but it worked.'

Some good news, finally, Rose thought.

Vincent seemed oblivious, staring morosely at the floor. Janine patted his shoulder. 'Don't fret, Master Vincent,' she said. 'You can recreate your inventions – your light bulbs and such. It may take a few years –'

'Decades,' Vincent said. 'But only Elspeth matters. She has no idea of the danger she's in.'

'What about the Patchwork Man?' Rose asked the Doctor. 'Can you make another Voltigrade trap?'

'That depends,' he said, and jabbed his elbow into Vincent's ribs. 'Oi, Vincent. Is there more equipment at the château?'

Vincent shot him a helpless look. 'My laboratory was *there*,' he said, pointing out of the window towards the fire on the horizon. 'The château is not set up for experiments.'

'Are there electric lights?' the Doctor asked. 'Copper wires? Chicken fencing? Iron?'

'Only lanterns,' Vincent said. 'No wires, no livestock. There may be some iron in the window frames; I'm afraid I can't recall.'

None of that sounded very useful. Rose met the Doctor's gaze.

'We'll think of something,' he said.

She wished she shared his confidence. 'Does the monster know where Elspeth is?'

Vincent thought about it and shook his head. 'Only that she's not in the manor.'

'How long will it take us to get to the château?' Rose asked.

Janine spoke up. 'Three hours, milady. Two, at this rate.'

The carriage was hurtling along the road awfully fast. Rose's teeth kept banging together inside her mouth. 'And on foot? A day or so?'

Janine shrugged. 'I suppose. Why?'

Rose suspected that the monster didn't need to rest, or eat. If he worked out where Elspeth was, he might reach the château only a few hours after they did. They didn't have long to come up with a new plan.

'So the fire didn't kill them,' she said slowly. 'But it broke them up – dispersed them, so they're harmless. Right?'

'Right,' the Doctor said.

'So could we do the same thing to the creature? Disperse it?'

'With what?'

Rose hesitated to suggest such a gruesome option, but it was the only thing she could think of: 'Dynamite?'

The Doctor looked appalled. 'Rose!'

'Why would I keep dynamite at my château?' Vincent asked reasonably.

Because you're a grave-robbing, monster-mashing lunatic, Rose thought, but didn't say.

'I don't know how we're going to fix this,' the Doctor said, 'but I know we're not going to do it with a bomb.'

Rose sighed. He was right, of course.

The carriage pressed on, the road growing rougher as they entered wilder country. Jagged mountains loomed up around them, wreathed in mist. The wind howled through narrow mountain passes as if crying out in pain. It was a bleak, unearthly landscape.

Despite the urgency of the situation, Rose found herself yawning. The events of the last two days were catching up with her. Soon, she felt herself starting to drift off, lulled by the rocking of the carriage.

She was perched on the edge of a dream – something about trying to explain to her mother that she didn't want to go to school with bolts in the sides of her neck, no matter what the new uniform guidelines said – when Vincent spoke, dragging her back up to consciousness.

'The coachman keeps his rifle in that trunk,' he said, nudging it with his foot.

'No bombs, no guns,' the Doctor said firmly. 'They just make bad situations worse.'

'Perhaps not in this case,' Vincent said. 'I believe the gun barrel is made of iron, and the shell casings are brass – which contains copper.'

The Doctor raised an eyebrow. 'Hmm. Worth investigating, I suppose.' He opened the trunk –

And Janine screamed.

There was no gun in the trunk. Instead, the coachman had been stuffed inside, his clothes too large for his shrivelled body. His sunken eyes stared up at Rose.

It took only a second for the sickening shock to become a terrifying realisation:

If the coachman was dead, who was driving the carriage?

The Runaway Carriage

Rose leapt up and threw open the carriage door, peering out into the stormy night. There, cloaked in shadow on the driver's bench, was a hulking figure wrapped in a horse blanket. He looked back at her, and lightning flashed, briefly illuminating his pale face, full of stitches and lumpy teeth.

'Best stay inside,' he said, grinning. 'We'll soon be at Loch Lamond.'

He whipped the reins, and the terrified horses galloped recklessly ahead.

Rose looked down at the rough stones flying past on either side of the muddy road. The carriage was going too quickly for anyone to leap out, which was probably the idea. She remembered, jarringly, that the creature's face had come from a man who died falling from a horse – under probably much less dangerous circumstances.

Lightning spidered across the sky, and the château was briefly visible on the horizon – a long, elegant building stretched over a narrow part of the loch. After the flash died away, Rose could still see the windows glowing like eyes.

Looking back into the carriage, Rose saw the horror on Vincent's face as he realised what he'd done. He'd told the creature exactly where Elspeth was. He had signed her death warrant.

'No,' he whispered. 'No, no, no!'

Rose had seen plenty of panicked people during her travels with the Doctor. She had learned not to wait for them to calm down. By then, it was usually too late. She ignored Vincent and grasped the Doctor's arm. 'What can we do?'

The Doctor drummed his fingers against the window. 'I'm thinking.'

'Think faster!' Rose said. She guessed the carriage would reach the château in less than an hour. At that point, the creature could barge inside and grab Elspeth before anyone in the carriage could stop him. He would suck the electrolytes out of her body before Vincent's eyes –

And then what? Once the creature had enjoyed his revenge, would he allow the Voltigrades to take over completely? Would he turn Rose and the others into shrunken dummies, or would some of them become hosts, like Bergam's two zombie friends?

Either way, they would all be doomed once they arrived at the château.

'Doctor,' she said. 'Can you slow us down?'

The Doctor produced his sonic and fiddled for a moment. The device had deceptively simple controls, but Rose had never quite grasped what it could and couldn't do. The Doctor had once tried to teach her how to open a jar with it.

She'd succeeded only in making her hair stand on end – for three days.

'Sorry,' the Doctor muttered, finally giving up. 'Horses don't have brakes.'

Worth a try, Rose thought. 'Fine. Let's do this the old-fashioned way.'

She grabbed the curtains with both hands and ripped them off the rail.

'What are you doing, miss?' Janine cried.

'Improvising.' Rose started tying the curtains together as though they were bedsheets and she was planning to escape through a prison window. Once she'd made the curtains into a rope, she tied one end through a ring bolt on the floor of the carriage and pulled the knot tight.

'I need something heavy – but smaller than this.' She held her fingers about ten centimetres apart.

A grin spread across the Doctor's face. 'I have no idea what you're planning, but I love it.'

Rose wasn't quite sure what she was planning either. She had only a wisp of an idea – but sometimes, she knew, that was enough.

Vincent produced his fob watch. 'This is heavy,' he said. 'It's eighteen-karat gold.'

Rose snatched it out of his hand. 'Perfect.' She tied the gold chain to the loose end of her curtain, then opened the door. The carriage filled with the sounds of clattering wheels, clopping hooves and booming thunder.

'The watch is quite fragile,' Vincent shouted. 'It was

passed down from my father to me, and from his father to him, on the occasion of —'

'Can't hear you,' Rose lied. 'Everybody hold on to something!'

She launched the rope outwards as though casting a fishing line, then pulled back on it, swinging the fob watch towards the rear wheel of the carriage.

The gold disc was just heavy enough. It disappeared between the spokes of the wheel. Immediately, the rope went taut, and the wheel stopped spinning, the rim skidding across the muddy road. The carriage swerved, almost throwing Rose out of the door, but she managed to hold on to the frame.

The creature wasn't so lucky. He was hurled sideways off the coachman's seat. He let out a bellow of rage as he sailed through the air, then hit the ground with a gruesome *thud*. Sparks exploded out of him — Voltigrades? — as his giant body bounced off the road and disappeared into a ditch.

Rose opened her mouth to cheer —

But then there was a sudden crack from beneath the floor of the carriage. It sounded like one of the axles snapping.

Sure enough, the wheel sagged, and then popped right off. The carriage lurched again, this time more violently. The rear corner descended into the mud as the opposite corner lifted into the air. The severed wheel rolled away until the rope went taut again, dragging it behind the tilted vehicle. The horses whinnied, terrified.

'Stop! Whoa!' Rose shouted at them, but, if anything, they seemed to speed up, their mighty hooves pounding the mud. The reins flapped loose behind them.

Everyone in the carriage yelled, clinging to their seat cushions to avoid being tossed around like coats in a tumble dryer. Rose blocked them all out. She had to stop the vehicle.

She climbed out of the open door and clung to the outside of the leaning carriage, her boots perched on the running board. Trees whipped past. The road was a deadly blur, less than half a metre beneath her feet. The sound of wood grinding along dirt was deafening. The carriage felt like it was shaking itself to bits. She gritted her teeth and climbed the ladder towards the coachman's empty seat, the wind tearing at her hair. The reins flapped wildly in the gale. She swiped for them, and missed.

Ahead, she saw a sharp bend in the road. The horses showed no sign of slowing down.

'Hold on!' Rose screamed to the others, not knowing if they could hear her, or if it even mattered. She swiped again and this time snagged the reins. She pulled as hard as she could, yelling, 'Woah! Woah!'

The horses slowed, but not enough. They took the corner so fast that the beams connected to their harnesses snapped.

Suddenly, the carriage was untethered. Rose let go of the reins just in time to avoid being wrenched off her seat. The horses galloped away, leaving the out-of-control carriage behind.

'Hold on!' she screamed again as the carriage hurtled off the road. The front corner clipped a tree, and the vehicle spun, flinging Rose sideways. She covered her face with her arms, flying blind.

And then the world went black.

The Tilted Mirror

'Rose?' the Doctor said. 'Can you hear me?'

Rose opened her eyes. She was somewhere dank and gloomy. It took a moment for her to recognise the murky ceiling of Vincent's laboratory. The cold steel under her back must be his examination table. The only sound was the clink and clatter of instruments against a tray.

Vincent himself loomed over her. 'Don't move,' he said. 'You'll tear your stitches.'

Stitches? Rose tried to speak, but her jaw wouldn't open. She couldn't turn her head, or even clench her fists.

'Rose?' the Doctor said again. He sounded distant, like he was in another room of the manor, searching for her.

'You'll be sore for a few days,' Vincent said. 'But I think we can declare the experiment a success.'

What experiment? The words echoed around her head but never reached her lips.

'Would you like to see?' Vincent asked. He held up a hand mirror as though he were a hairdresser asking if she was happy with the length at the back.

Rose saw her own frightened eyes. As Vincent tilted the

mirror downwards, she realised there was a line of ragged stitches across her throat. They seemed to go all the way round her neck.

No, she thought.

Vincent tilted the mirror further. The rest of Rose's body was revealed, but it wasn't her own body. There was a man's hand, a woman's leg, a young stomach and an old hairy knee, all threaded together in a quilt of nightmares –

'No!' she screamed, and sat bolt upright.

She suddenly felt the rain in her hair and the cold breeze on her skin. She wasn't in the manor. It had burned down, she now remembered. She was in a pile of leaf litter, mud under her legs. The carriage lay on its side several metres away, half-smashed against a thick oak tree. The doors had broken off, and the interior was empty. She could hear the rustling of trees and the faint flap of bat wings.

'Rose!' The Doctor was crouched next to her. 'Are you all right?'

Rose looked down at her body. Her own hands were peeking out of Elspeth's clothes. She felt her throat. No stitches.

'Fine,' she said, willing her heart to stop racing. 'Just a nightmare.'

The Doctor looked far from reassured. After all the things he'd seen and done, Rose couldn't imagine what *his* nightmares were like.

Rose thought dreams were a glimpse into the brain's recycling bin. One last chance to check that there was nothing important among the jumbled rubbish, before the truck came to take it all away. If she had dreamed about being stitched together, maybe that meant her brain had rejected some of the things she'd seen over the last two days. But the nightmare had also given her some sympathy for the creature. She'd literally seen things from his perspective – waking up on Vincent's table, confused, frightened, her body unfamiliar. She could imagine how quickly her fear and helplessness might become rage at Dr Frankenstein, the man who had done this to her.

The Doctor put his sonic back in his pocket. 'No sign of concussion.' He stood, offering his hand. 'You were only out for a few minutes.'

'Felt longer,' Rose grumbled, letting him help her to her feet. 'Where are Vincent and Janine?'

The Doctor pointed through the trees to the road. 'They took off towards the château,' he said. 'I think we should get after them. Can you walk?'

Rose stood. She was a little woozy, but nothing felt broken or even bruised. She'd been very lucky. 'Yeah. Let's go.'

She kept her gaze on the forest as they jogged back towards the road. The creature had probably survived the fall from the cart – from what she could gather, the Voltigrades would keep it animated no matter what. Rose hoped that she and the Doctor wouldn't have to terminate the creature's unnatural life. But she truly couldn't see another way for this to end.

The Secret Passage

The rain had eased, the clouds had receded and the moon looked down on them like a giant milky eye. It was just bright enough to follow Vincent's and Janine's footprints along the muddy track.

Just as Rose's legs started to give way, the forest opened out and the château came into view in the distance. It was bigger than the manor had been, with probably dozens of rooms. Lamplight flickered behind mullioned windows. The building was perched atop a cliff as though it had grown from the rock, the wrought-iron balconies overlooking the loch, where the moonlight glittered on the water.

Rose rested her palms on her thighs, gasping for air. 'It looks . . . like Colin . . . Firth's house.'

The Doctor didn't even sound out of breath. 'You mean *Mr Darcy's* house. Colin's place is nothing like . . . Hang on, I know this place! There's an excellent guided tour, but the next one isn't scheduled to start for another –' he checked his watch – 'seventy-seven years.'

'Did the guide tell you anything useful? Emergency exits, that kind of thing?'

The Doctor scratched his chin. 'Hmm. I can't quite –'

'Never mind. No time.' Rose forced herself to run again, down the crumbling stone path towards the gates. Ominously, they stood wide open.

The Doctor examined the handle. 'No lock,' he observed.

Rose could see why Vincent had been so terrified that the creature would discover Elspeth was here. This place really was defenceless.

'But Vincent and Janine would have closed the gates behind them, surely?' Rose whispered.

The Doctor's eyes narrowed. Rose could guess what he was thinking: *not if they knew the Patchwork Man was already inside*.

If the creature had arrived first, everyone in the château was probably dead. This thing could kill with a single touch. Even a two-hearted being like the Doctor was unlikely to survive the draining of every cell in his body.

Rose thought about asking him if they should go back to the TARDIS. But she was afraid he would say no – and then she was afraid he would say yes. How was she supposed to go home, knowing she'd abandoned these people?

The Doctor shot her a questioning look.

Rose steeled herself. They had never given up on an adventure, and they wouldn't start now. She nodded.

The Doctor's face broke into a grin, and then he put a finger to his lips. She nodded again, and they both tiptoed through the open gate, towards the front door.

The door was thick oak banded with iron, like an old barrel. It featured a tough-looking lock, hard to get through –

except that the door, like the gate, stood wide open. They looked at one another, then slipped inside into the dark.

The foyer was lit by wall-mounted lanterns, which were just about the only intact items in sight. Broken vases, torn curtains and splintered furniture were scattered across the marble floor. Dirty footprints led towards a wide staircase. Rose's faint hope that the creature hadn't yet arrived was immediately snuffed out.

She gestured to the stairs and made an *after you* motion. The Doctor nodded grimly and started climbing.

At the top, a long hallway stretched before them, doors on either side hanging off their hinges. Had the creature smashed in all these doors, looking for Elspeth? Rose didn't see any bodies, but a horrible, deathly silence hung over everything. Rose had once visited an Aztec tomb with the Doctor. What she remembered most – other than the knee-deep dust and desiccated spiders dangling like miniature chandeliers – was this same suffocating absence of noise.

They crept down the hallway, peering cautiously into each ransacked room. Shattered glass and overturned furniture bore testament to the creature's rampage. Rose was beginning to lose hope when a faint sound caught her attention – a muffled whisper.

She whirled round.

'What is it?' the Doctor asked.

Rose shushed him. It had been so faint that she might have imagined it. She stood still, ears straining. She closed her eyes, which may have been dangerous in this situation, but always seemed to make her ears work better.

It was no use. The sound was not repeated.

She opened her eyes again. The Doctor looked at her expectantly.

'Thought I heard a whisper,' she said. 'But it must have been the wind.'

'What wind?' the Doctor asked.

He was right. The château was well-built, and they'd closed the front door behind them. There were no draughts anywhere.

Rose looked around. 'When he was making his monster,' she said slowly, 'Vincent used the brains of two rich guys who died duelling each other. Right?'

'Right,' the Doctor confirmed.

'And the creature can talk, and even write. No one taught it, so it must have inherited its knowledge.'

'Stands to reason,' the Doctor agreed. 'What are you thinking?'

'It's searched the bedrooms.' Rose gestured at the trashed corridor. 'And the bathroom and the dining room. It probably believes it's searched the whole house. But rich people don't think about the lives of their servants. They might not even wonder how they get from room to room so fast.'

'Rose Tyler,' the Doctor said slowly. 'I think you might be brilliant.'

They both turned slowly in opposite directions to look at the same bare wall. It was between two open doors, and the rooms beyond didn't seem quite big enough.

Rose pressed her ear to the wallpaper. There was a long

moment of silence and then a sound that might have been a muted sob.

'Hello?' she called softly.

There was a tiny squeak of terror.

'It's Rose and the Doctor,' Rose said. 'We're here to help, I promise.'

For a long moment, there was only silence. Then came the scraping of furniture being moved aside. Part of the wall swung slightly inwards, revealing a sliver of a pale, frightened face.

'Janine,' Rose said, relieved.

'Miss Rose.' There were tears in Janine's eyes. 'It's here.'

'I know,' Rose said. 'Is anyone with you?'

Janine opened the door a little wider. Crammed into the narrow corridor between rooms, Rose could see Janine and several other people, along with the wooden box they'd used to brace the door. The men wore plain black clothes; the women were in white aprons. These must be the servants at the château.

'Is everyone okay?' Rose asked.

'It's here,' Janine repeated. 'It was smashing in doors . . .'

Rose stood on tiptoes to scan the faces behind Janine. 'Is Elspeth with you? Or Vincent?'

Janine shook her head vigorously. 'No. It saw us and we ran, and I thought Master Vincent – excuse me, Dr Frankenstein – was right behind me, but when I turned they were both gone, and I didn't know what to do, then Gerald . . .' She gestured at one of the men in black. 'He was in here already, so he opened the door and let me in.'

'The path to the front door is clear,' the Doctor said. 'You should all go. Head for the village as fast as you can.'

The man behind Janine, Gerald, spoke up. 'But what if that . . . that *thing* comes after us?'

'It won't.' The Doctor looked further up the corridor, towards the wing of the house they hadn't yet explored. 'Not until it has Elspeth.'

Rose suspected that he was right. The Voltigrades and the monster had overlapping agendas – the Voltigrades were hungry, and the creature wanted revenge. Once the Voltigrades had consumed Elspeth and Vincent, the monster would be satisfied, but the Voltigrades wouldn't. They'd come after everyone else in the house.

'How do you –'

Janine shushed Gerald. 'You can trust these two,' she said. 'They know what they're doing.'

Rose was flattered. She really had no idea what she was doing; she only knew what was *going on*. This, admittedly, put her a step ahead of the château staff, but she didn't have a plan and wasn't sure the Doctor did, either.

All the more reason to get these people to safety.

'Get out,' she told them. 'While you still can.'

Those six ominous words seemed to do the trick. The servants scrambled out of their hidey-hole so fast they nearly trampled each other hurrying down the stairs towards the front door.

Janine was last. She hesitated, turning to the Doctor and Rose. 'Save Dr Frankenstein,' she begged. 'Please.'

'We'll try. Go!' Rose hated the thought of her new friend staying in danger a second longer than she had to.

Janine didn't move. 'He's not a bad man,' she insisted.

'I know,' Rose said. Vincent was mad, perhaps, but not bad. He hadn't known Voltigrades existed. He couldn't have foreseen the terrible consequences of his experiment.

'Don't worry,' the Doctor said. 'I have a plan. You get the others to a safe distance, all right?'

Janine looked satisfied. She clenched her fists and ran.

Rose watched her go, listening to the flurry of receding footsteps. Eventually the front door boomed, and that same deathly silence fell.

'Do you *actually* have a plan?' she asked.

'I *will* have one,' the Doctor said, 'by the time we find the monster.'

'So you lied.'

'Of course not. I just accidentally used the present tense instead of the future tense. English is a tricky language for a time traveller.'

'Mm-hmm,' Rose said, not believing him for a minute. 'Come on, then. It's time to save the Bride of Frankenstein.'

They made their way through the labyrinthine, gloomy hallways of the old château. Despite her best efforts to tread lightly, Rose's boots scuffed against the ornate rugs and the worn stone floor, each step echoing through the still air and bouncing off high ceilings.

The sonic hummed as the Doctor held it aloft. Its ethereal blue glow threw long shadows across toppled statues and shredded paintings. Every creak of aged timber or rustle of unseen vermin made Rose jump.

A little moonlight had filtered through the tall windows, but soon it faded to nothing. A moment later, rain spattered the glass. Thunder boomed. The storm was back with a vengeance.

'If I were a collection of body parts possessed by a sentient colony of electrons,' the Doctor murmured thoughtfully, 'where would I hide?'

'Why would it be hiding?' Rose whispered. 'We're not much of a threat.' The Doctor had already told her that the creature couldn't be killed, and in any case, their only weapon was a screwdriver.

'If it's not hiding,' the Doctor said, 'then where is it?'

They reached a set of carved wooden doors and pushed them open, the hinges creaking ominously. Beyond lay a cavernous ballroom, the parquet floor littered with shattered ceramic and crystal.

There was still no sign of the creature, or anyone.

Rose hesitated. 'Maybe it's lying in wait. Ready to ambush us. Or ambush Elspeth?'

The Doctor seemed like he was about to answer when a terrible scream rang out from the French windows at the far end of the ballroom.

The Doctor and Rose ran, glass crunching beneath their shoes. The French windows were open, billowing curtains revealing a stone balcony overlooking the misty grounds. There, silhouetted against the moon-scorched clouds, stood the monster.

Adam

The Patchwork Man's clothes were torn, his pallid flesh slick with rain. One gloved hand clutched Elspeth's throat, holding her over the edge of the balcony, a hundred metres above the loch. She struggled feebly, eyes wide with terror. Her breaths came in panicked gasps. Rose remembered all too well how it felt to have those huge fingers round her neck.

'Let her go,' the Doctor shouted, as he burst through the French doors.

'*After* pulling her back on to the balcony,' Rose quickly added.

The monster turned to face them, eyes glowing blue. 'You,' he said.

'Us,' the Doctor agreed, brandishing his sonic.

'Elspeth,' Rose said. 'Are you all right?'

The pretty woman gave a helpless gurgle in the monster's grip.

'Not yet,' the monster muttered, as if to himself. 'You cannot have her yet. No!'

Rose guessed he was speaking to the Voltigrades inside his head.

'Put – her – down,' the Doctor said.

The creature eyed the sonic screwdriver. 'I have no fear of your little flashing light.'

'Maybe not, but *They* won't like it.' The Doctor's jaw was set, his eyes dark with determination. Rose hoped he was telling the truth, but suspected he was bluffing.

The monster looked at them for a long moment.

'Very well,' he said finally. He swung round, lifting Elspeth back over the banister and gently lowered her to the floor –

Then he launched himself at the Doctor.

He was quick, but the Doctor was quicker, flicking a switch on the screwdriver as he backed away. The monster roared, lashing out with one huge arm. As his hand neared the sonic, the device did something Rose had never seen before. Its whine became a squeal, and the usually faint glow became a bright flash. Then, it went dark.

The Doctor clicked helplessly at the switch, but the screwdriver did not respond. It had shut itself down when something started to drain its energy.

The monster had a faint blue glow around his fingertips. He smacked his scarred lips and bared his lumpy yellow teeth in a gruesome approximation of a smile. 'On the contrary, *We* enjoyed that very much.'

Elspeth crawled along the floor towards the French windows, retching. She didn't look capable of running.

Rose faced the creature. 'Listen to me. I've seen a lot of versions of you on the telly. I know what happens next.'

'You know nothing,' the creature growled, and the stone

balcony vibrated beneath Rose's feet. The cold blue glow burned brighter behind his eyes, so bright it hurt to meet his gaze, but Rose dared not look away.

'Your revenge gives you no joy,' she told him. 'Frankenstein hunts you for the rest of his life. When he dies, you go mad with grief. That's how the story ends.' She hoped she was remembering it right.

The Doctor seemed to think so. 'Spoiler warning,' he murmured.

The glow in the creature's eyes flickered. Rose realised that the Voltigrade colony was struggling to maintain control. *That's it*, she thought. *Fight them!*

'This is not a story,' the monster snarled.

'It is,' Rose insisted. 'But it's *your* story. You get to choose the ending, Adam.'

The monster blinked, startled. Rose had thought someone else had used the name earlier, but perhaps she was wrong. Maybe it had come from one of the Frankenstein movies she'd seen. Maybe the creature had been susceptible to the whispers of the Voltigrades because everyone had called it 'the creature' instead of recognising him as a man.

'It is too late,' he said.

'Never,' the Doctor said gently.

'*Look at me*,' roared the monster – Adam. Eyes flickering, sputtering, he gestured with a mighty hand at his hulking, unnatural form. 'I am no man! I am mere . . . parts!'

'We all are,' Rose said. 'Parts of our parents, parts of our past, lots of little, you know, cells and stuff . . .' She glanced at the Doctor, wanting him to take over.

He was better at sciencey things. But he just gave her an encouraging nod.

'. . . but when all those parts come together,' Rose went on, 'we get to choose what they do.'

Adam thrust a quivering finger at her. 'I did not ask for this life! Dr Frankenstein forced it upon me!'

'Yeah, that's what parents do,' Rose said. 'But it's not up to them to decide how you live it. And those things inside you, *they* don't get to decide either.'

'You know nothing,' Adam repeated.

Rose opened her mouth, but found she had no more words to attempt to convince him. She'd done her best. But the well of inspiration was dry.

'And yet,' Adam said finally, 'you know so much.' A glowing blue tear rolled down his cheek.

Rose smiled. 'I had a good teacher.'

The Doctor modestly waved off the compliment.

'My mum,' Rose added.

Adam let out a long, shuddering sigh that seemed to deflate his hulking frame. He turned his gaze to the dark sky, observing the swirling clouds. More tears fell from his chin, sparking against the stone floor.

For a long moment, no one said anything. Then Adam pointed upward. 'That's where They come from, is it not? The lightning?'

'That's right,' Rose said.

Adam put his palms to the sides of his head. 'They say I'm weak,' he moaned. 'Pathetic. A poor host.'

'We can get them out.' The Doctor looked down at the

dead screwdriver. 'I don't suppose you can undo what they did to this? Because it takes quite a while to charge, you see, and . . .'

Rose wasn't listening. She was watching Adam's fingers, which had started to twitch. Even Adam didn't seem to notice as the movement spread to his hand, which clenched and unclenched as though grabbing for something.

'Um, Doctor?' Rose said.

The Doctor stopped mid-sentence, noticing Adam staring at him intently. There was something unsettling about the creature's gaze. It made Rose's skin crawl.

'Adam?' the Doctor asked. 'Are you all right?'

The convulsions had spread to Adam's arm now. He still didn't seem to notice. 'Never better,' he said, smiling.

'What are you feeling?'

'I'm *hearing*,' Adam said. His eyes were glowing again. 'The two hearts beating in your chest. What an . . . *interesting* biological anomaly.'

The Doctor's expression hardened. 'Listen to me,' he said. 'These aren't your thoughts.'

Adam walked closer, transfixed. His eyes blazed brighter and brighter. 'Two hearts pumping lifeblood through your veins.'

Rose looked on in horror as Adam's frame swelled before her eyes. Buttons flew off his tattered shirt, exposing his chest. His skin rippled and pulsed like a thousand worms were writhing beneath his flesh.

'This isn't you,' she cried.

'She's right.' The Doctor was backing away. 'It's the

Voltigrade colony trying to reassert itself. You can't let them win. Understand?'

The worms bubbled up, a seething mass of energy and flesh. When Adam spoke next, it was as though he had a dozen voices, all speaking in unison: 'What a powerful host you would be.'

Rose saw it all, then. The Voltigrades would take over the Doctor's seemingly invincible body. They would gain access to his knowledge. They would use the TARDIS to consume not only all the organic life on this planet in this time, but on *all* planets in *all* times.

She found herself moving towards Adam, like she could block his path to the Doctor. But Adam was twice her size, and if she touched his skin, she would be drained.

'Fight it, Adam!' The Doctor raised his lightless sonic screwdriver. He must have known it would do nothing to the creature, but the Doctor was like that. Hopeful to the very end.

Adam picked up speed.

So did Rose, charging towards him.

'Rose!' the Doctor shouted. 'Don't!'

But Rose had already thrown herself forward, shielding her face with her arms. She slammed into the Patchwork Man, who grunted, startled. Rose managed to get a grip on his shirt as he staggered sideways –

Then they both tumbled over the balcony.

The Falling Pair

Rose had always suspected it would end like this. That she would never retire from travelling with the Doctor, but have just one more adventure, and then one more after that, over and over until one of them died. But she had assumed the Doctor would sacrifice his life to save hers, not the other way around.

There were endless ways to rationalise what she'd done. The Doctor had saved so many lives. He didn't deserve to become a host for something that could do untold damage across time and space. Even if it simply killed him, that would leave the Earth, and the universe, defenceless when the next alien threat arrived, be it Daleks, Slitheen or some other unknown horror.

But as she and the creature tumbled over the railing and plummeted towards the loch, Rose's choice didn't feel like a choice at all. All the parts of her had sprung into action – her legs running, her arms reaching out – without waiting for her brain to decide.

Maybe she'd been wrong when she'd told Adam that he could choose. *Maybe*, she thought, *we just are who we are.*

Even as her mind was racing through these thoughts, like a crash course in philosophy, her body was grappling with Adam in mid-air, trying to keep a hold of his clothes without touching his skin. It was a long way down, and when she hit the water, the impact would surely kill her. If it didn't, she would surely freeze, and even if *that* didn't happen, she would drown, unable to swim in Elspeth's heavy petticoats. But that didn't mean she was willing to get explosively dehydrated and dummified on the way down.

They fell faster and faster, the wind ripping the air from Rose's lungs so that she couldn't even scream. Adam thrashed in her grip like a mighty shark, bellowing, but Rose couldn't make out any words over the blasting gale. She *could* hear a dark chittering, though – a disturbing sound that made her itchy all over. The Voltigrades, straining to get at her.

It was probably safest to let go of him, but she couldn't. The thought of having nothing to hang on to as she fell towards the loch made her sick with terror.

As they plummeted, the creature managed to grab Rose with one of his huge hands. He hugged her tightly, her cheek against his exposed collarbone, and Rose felt it. The Voltigrades, swarming on to her bare skin like living sparks. Her flesh tingled painfully as they burrowed in, spreading through her cells.

'No!' she shrieked, as she felt the Voltigrade colony spread to every cell in her body –

But it didn't drain her. It *filled* her. Rose suddenly felt strong, like she could kick down a door or lift a car. All her muscles crackled with strength. Her senses were heightened, too. She could hear gentle lapping sounds from the shoreline, hundreds of metres away. The darkness no longer mattered – she could see the Doctor high above, leaning over the railing. She could make out the individual hairs on his outstretched wrists and the veins in his frantic eyes.

Rose felt a wild grin spread across her face.

And then she heard someone whispering, not in her ear but in her mind. It was Them.

You like this, yes?

They spoke in Rose's own voice, which should have been creepy. But all her fear was gone. She was falling towards certain death, and yet, she felt invincible.

You will be our host. You will take us to the Time Lord.

A distant corner of Rose's mind wondered how these parasites knew what a Time Lord was, and then she realised they must have plucked the knowledge out of her head.

He will trust you, They said.

'Fight them,' Adam shouted. 'Fight them, wise girl!'

They seemed to have left his body to take over hers. Rose ignored him. Why would she want to fight this? She'd never, *ever* felt this good.

'Yes,' she told Them. 'I will take you to the Doctor.'

Then they hit the water.

The Empty Lungs

The creature landed on his back, and Rose landed on top of him. He broke her fall, but it was like getting hit by a train made of steak. She had the wind knocked out of her, and then they both went under. The freezing water rushed in, pummelling Rose from all sides at once. It felt like a thousand knives of ice stabbing at every inch of exposed skin, and a split second later Elspeth's clothes were soaked, and the cold reached her *un*exposed skin, too. Rose had visited the North Pole, the South Pole and the darkest regions of space, but she'd never felt cold like this. It was pitch black, and she couldn't work out which way was up.

Screams filled her head. Not her own screams, but Theirs. The colony was being torn apart. Rose felt their shock, their agony, their confusion. *What is happening? What trickery is this?* Suddenly, the water around her became warm, and then hot. It boiled, as the microscopic parasites were ripped out of her skin. But how? By what?

Then there was silence. She was alone in her head once more.

One of her grasping hands felt air and then lost it just as quickly. The crash-landing had taken her deep underwater, but the saltwater had made her buoyant, and she'd already floated back up. She splashed around, trying to find the surface again. She didn't feel invincible any more. Her empty lungs were burning. She needed air, *now*, but she couldn't find it, and she was tangled in the folds of this ridiculous dress. The warmth from the escaping Voltigrades was dissipating.

'Doctor!' she screamed, the last of her breath coming out as a stream of bubbles. She couldn't imagine a universe in which he didn't save her. Whatever the planet, whatever the century, whenever she'd needed him, he'd been there for her.

She flung out both her arms, reaching for something, *anything* –

And strong hands found hers.

Rose found herself dragged on to the broad back of someone who set off for the shoreline with a powerful stroke. Perhaps, when they got on to dry land, the Doctor would reveal that he'd trained as an Olympic swimmer, or something.

But when they reached the stony beach, Rose realised she hadn't been rescued by the Doctor, but by the creature. Adam.

Her Voltigrade-enhanced night vision was gone, but she could see him well enough to tell that he looked different. His eyes were brown rather than electric blue. He was sagging, exhausted after the swim, where previously he'd seemed to have impossible strength. The shelf bracket had fallen off him at some point, probably because his body was no longer magnetic. His expression was sad – but utterly human.

'Are you all right?' he asked her. His voice was different. Uncertain, frail.

'Yeah,' she said. 'Are *you* all right?'

'I'm . . .' He looked down at his big hands. 'No. I don't think I am.' He buried his face in the crook of his elbow. He didn't seem so frightening now.

'What's . . .?' Rose trailed off. She knew exactly what was wrong, because she felt it too. The loss of the Voltigrades. She'd been so powerful, and now she was just a person again.

'It's okay,' she told Adam.

'It is not.' He looked up and the hopelessness in his eyes broke her heart. 'I have killed.'

Oh. He was feeling something different to her.

'That wasn't you,' she said. 'It was Them. The Voltigrades.'

'It *was* me,' Adam insisted. 'I remember doing those monstrous things. I remember *deciding* to do them.'

Rose remembered the brief period when the Voltigrades had infested her mind. How quickly she'd decided to betray the Doctor.

Feeling faintly sick, she looked towards the château just in time to see the Doctor emerge. He looked around, spotted them and ran in their direction. Vincent and Elspeth were right behind him, holding hands as they hurried along.

How can I tell him? she wondered. *How can I not?*

Rose took Adam's hand. Despite the cold of the water, his flesh was warm, like a fresh loaf of bread. He felt like a person now.

'It wasn't you,' she said firmly. 'It wasn't either of us. Okay?'

Tears filled Adam's eyes. 'What am I to do?' he asked. 'I have nothing. I am welcome nowhere. My features . . .' He gestured at his face and body. 'No one will ever accept what

I am. I cannot even accept it myself. Am I to haunt this forest forever?'

It did seem like an impossible situation. But the Doctor was nearly here.

And impossible situations were the Doctor's speciality.

The Giant Puddle

'Fantastic!' the Doctor shouted as he approached. 'Rose Tyler, you're a genius!'

Rose coughed, a mist of brine exploding from her lungs. 'Yeah,' she agreed. 'But . . . why?'

'You found a giant puddle!' the Doctor exclaimed. 'Better yet, a salty one! Irresistible to those little critters. It pulled them right out!' He gestured at Adam, who was sitting on the stony beach, hugging his knees. 'The whole loch is a Voltigrade trap! Like Janine said – any problem can be solved with a bath.'

It was both touching and infuriating that he thought Rose had expected this to happen. In reality, she'd simply been trying to save his life.

This realisation helped her to forgive herself. Yes, she'd thought about betraying the Doctor – but before the Voltigrades entered her body, she'd been willing to die to save him. The betrayal had been theirs, not hers.

Vincent and Elspeth arrived, both out of breath. When Vincent saw that Adam was weeping, he hesitated for only a moment before he crouched and passed a silk handkerchief to the giant. Adam took it, but simply held it, tears streaming unchecked down his cheeks. They weren't glowing any more. After a moment, Vincent took the handkerchief back and gently wiped away Adam's tears.

Rose remembered something Vincent had said in his laboratory: *I need my father to teach me how to be a husband, and how to raise my children.* Something told her Vincent would do just fine.

'I am so sorry,' Adam told his maker, his big head sagging.

'The folly was mine,' Vincent said, 'and mine alone.'

The Doctor watched all of this with interest. He reminded Rose of David Attenborough, studying a family of rare birds. Come to think of it, Rose had never seen him and Attenborough in the same room – and even if she had, that wouldn't prove anything. The Doctor had said that as a time traveller he sometimes ended up in the same room as himself.

Elspeth took Rose's hand and smiled. 'I told you Vincent was a good man.'

'You were right,' Rose conceded. 'Though he seems to get a bit carried away sometimes.'

Elspeth waved this off. 'All men have hobbies,' she said airily. 'Never fear – he shan't have time for grave-robbing once we are blessed with children.'

'Oh, good,' Rose said queasily. She wondered if Elspeth was just as barmy as her husband-to-be.

Edging away from her, Rose asked the Doctor, 'Is it safe to stand this close to the loch?'

'Hmm?' The Doctor sounded surprised. 'Why wouldn't it be?'

Rose boggled at him. She knew the Doctor could be forgetful, but this had happened only minutes ago. 'Because of the colony of electrical parasites in it.'

'Oh, *that*.' The Doctor beamed. 'Remember what I said? Voltigrades don't come together naturally. They were *forced* together. Now the saltwater has dispersed them, there's no reason for them to become a single conscious entity again. They're perfectly happy in microscopic form, as long as they have plenty of electrolytes to eat. A body of salty water this size should keep them fed for . . .' He counted on his fingers, muttered, 'Carry the three,' and then finished: 'Eight quintillion years.'

'Oh,' Rose said. She had mixed feelings about the Voltigrades being happy.

The Doctor sensed her discomfort. 'You can't blame them, Rose,' he said. 'They did what was in their nature.'

Rose nodded, and smiled. 'And we did what was in ours.'

The Doctor put an arm round her shoulders. 'Exactly.'

Behind them, Vincent cried out in horror.

Everyone whirled round. 'What?' Rose demanded.

'I forgot!' Vincent said. 'The wedding!'

The Wedding Guest

Two days later, the quaint village church was adorned with flowering vines and pink roses. Inside, sunlight streamed through the stained-glass windows, casting a rainbow across the waiting pews. The guests were a strange assortment of farmers, nobles, academics and assorted oddballs. An old sea captain was telling tall tales to anyone who would listen. Janine was bustling around, hugging people. She had no official role, and had been promoted from servant to guest.

Vincent's bruises had faded, his cuts scabbed over. He looked resplendent in a black velvet suit as he waited by the altar.

The Doctor eyed him from their spot near the back of the church. 'Do you think I could pull off a bow-tie?' he whispered to Rose. 'I've often thought about it.'

Rose shushed him.

With everything that had happened, Rose might have expected Vincent and Elspeth to postpone their wedding. But Vincent had been aghast at the suggestion.

'We very nearly died,' he'd said. 'How could we possibly wait a moment longer?'

'Life is short,' Elspeth had agreed, squeezing his hand.

'Wouldn't you rather get married when things have settled down a bit?' Rose asked. 'Rather than two days after your house burned to the ground?'

Vincent chortled. 'To be honest, I got off lightly. At the reception, you should ask my brother about his bachelor party.'

Rose had been surprised when the Doctor accepted the invitation. He liked to vanish as soon as the crisis was resolved, perhaps knowing there was a universe full of other desperate souls waiting for his help.

She nudged him with her elbow. 'Do you like weddings?'

He shrugged. 'Flowers, cake, dancing. What's not to like?'

Rose caught something in his tone. 'Have you ever been married?' she asked curiously.

He shushed her. 'The ceremony is about to start.'

Guests streamed into the church. Rose overheard just enough conversation to identify a couple of Vincent's childhood friends, Elspeth's beloved grandparents, a handful of jovial uncles and wise aunts. It wasn't a big wedding, but it looked to be a happy one.

A wheezy old organ fired up, sounding not unlike the TARDIS. The guests stood. Two bridesmaids entered, dressed in butter-yellow dresses and carrying bouquets of baby's breath. They were smiling anxiously – Rose wondered what, if anything, they'd been told about the events of the last few days.

Elspeth glided in, holding the elbow of a stooped, beaming man who was presumably her father. She wore a simple blue gown with delicate beadwork along the neckline, her smile glowing behind the veil. All eyes were on her – except Rose's. Rose had noticed something behind her – a giant shadow in the open doorway.

Vincent had invited Adam to the ceremony, and Adam had refused, muttering something about being unholy and unable to enter a house of God. Vincent hadn't pushed, presumably knowing that the guests would run screaming if they saw him. Apparently, Adam had decided to observe from a safe distance.

When Elspeth reached the altar, Rose quickly squeezed past the Doctor and slipped away to the back of the church. Sure, Adam couldn't come in, but that didn't mean he had to be alone.

'Beautiful day,' he murmured without looking at her.

'I'm glad you came,' Rose whispered. Part of her had worried that he would follow his character arc in the story after all, and head for the North Pole.

'Of course,' Adam said stiffly. 'It is my father's wedding.'

She had never heard him refer to Vincent as his father, but she supposed it was appropriate.

The ceremony was brief. 'You may now kiss the bride,' the vicar said. The guests cheered as Vincent and Elspeth fell into each other's arms.

Adam watched with a complicated look on his face.

Rose guessed what he was thinking. She touched his hand. 'You'll find someone,' she said. 'Who sees past the stitches.'

'Indeed,' Adam said, not believing her, but too proud to say so.

Rose couldn't blame him. She tried to imagine how he would ever find love. Maybe he could chat up a woman at a Halloween party, and after he'd won her over reveal that he wasn't wearing a costume?

'I think your new stepmother likes you,' she said.

'Elspeth has no children of her own. Come next summer, I suspect I shall be relegated to the role of manservant . . .' Adam cleared his throat and forced a smile. 'Forgive me. Now that my thoughts are my own, they have developed the habit of escaping past my lips.'

Rose's heart panged. He was right, of course. Two of her friends had doted on their dog until they'd had a baby and pushed the pet out into the cold, lonely back garden.

'I'm sorry,' she said. 'I can't think of anything to say to make you feel better.'

'You have listened,' Adam replied. 'It is enough.'

Rose tried to imagine going back to the TARDIS and leaving Adam behind so she and the Doctor could go gallivanting off with the transhumanists on Tyronica Prime. She wouldn't feel good about it. Nor would the Doctor, she was sure. Even the TARDIS would probably object via silent disobedience. In fact . . .

Rose's eyes widened. She'd solved the final mystery.

'Excuse me a moment,' she said, and hurried back up the aisle. She grabbed the Doctor's shoulder, startling him.

'What is it?' he asked.

'I know why we're here,' she said.

'Really? I've met monks much older than you who are still grappling with that question.'

'No! I mean, I know why the TARDIS brought us here.'

The Doctor frowned. 'To save Earth from the Voltigrades, surely?'

'No,' Rose said. 'To give Adam a lift.'

A broad grin spread across the Doctor's face. 'Like I said. Rose Tyler: fantastic.'

The Blue Box

'I don't understand,' said Vincent as they approached the TARDIS. A welcoming light glowed on top, guiding them to it.

'You don't need to,' Rose said. 'It's a *really* long story.'

'And we don't want to be late,' the Doctor added, though Rose knew he could arrive at any time he liked.

The Doctor twisted the key and pushed the door open. 'Hop in, Adam.'

Adam's gigantic form was silhouetted against the setting sun. He studied the box warily. 'I'll not fit,' he said, embarrassed.

The Doctor smiled. 'Trust me.'

'How does the light work?' Vincent marvelled. 'There are no power lines.'

'*That's* the part that amazes you?' Rose asked. 'You're not wondering how we intend to travel?'

Vincent touched the side of the box. 'Surely this – outhouse? – isn't large enough to contain a battery that could keep the globe illuminated.'

Rose rolled her eyes. She was getting bored of the past

and looking forward to the future. 'Yeah, you can go now, Vince. We'll take it from here.'

'Elspeth is waiting,' the Doctor added.

Vincent blushed and cleared his throat. 'Well, yes. Quite right.' He turned and held out his hand to Adam. 'I am . . . honoured to be your father.'

Adam shook it. 'And I to be your son.'

Rose's eyes stung. It seemed impossible that these two would ever meet again. But if any nineteenth-century human was likely to end up on another planet in another time, she supposed it was Dr Frankenstein.

Adam straightened his spine, smoothed his ragged clothes and stepped through the door. Rose waited for him to walk right back out and go around, wondering how it could be so big on the inside, but he didn't.

The Doctor noticed this, too. 'After all that electricity, it's probably hard to shock him,' he joked. He followed Adam in.

Rose was the last through the door. She paused in the doorway and turned back to Vincent, who was looking more and more perplexed. 'Don't worry,' she promised. 'He'll be happy among his own kind, and we'll get him there safely.'

'But . . . how?' Vincent asked.

Rose smiled. 'Just watch,' she said, closing the door.

Inside, Adam was examining the controls, his big hands behind his back.

'Quite a ship, Doctor,' he said.

'You don't know the half of it.' The Doctor circled the central console, pushing buttons and throwing levers.

'And it can truly take us to this new world?'

'We'll be there in minutes,' the Doctor promised.

'Unless she decides to make another stop,' Rose put in. 'To pick up Humpty Dumpty or something.'

The Doctor shot her a stern look, but she could tell he was amused.

Adam looked down at his big hands. He swallowed before speaking. 'Can you be sure they will accept me?'

The Doctor smiled. 'You're not as different as you think, Adam. Rose told you – we're all bits of this and pieces of that. Strands of our parents' DNA, cells from the things we eat, energy that comes, ultimately, from whatever star we were born closest to. All these things come together to make us, and for a single, fantastic moment, we are who we are. Then we die and all our bits and pieces are released, free to become part of something else.'

Like an alien David Attenborough, Rose thought. But she loved travelling with him.

'When you think about it,' she said, 'we're all just parts. I don't mean we're *made* of parts – I mean we're parts of bigger things. You could say the whole Earth is alive, and we're just cells in its body.'

'You could,' the Doctor agreed softly, and Rose remembered that his own planet was gone.

He was holding the final lever. Rose reached out and put her hand over his.

'And none of us is alone,' he said, smiling.

She smiled back. 'On to the next adventure?'

'Always,' he said, and pulled down the lever.

Acknowledgements

Thank you to my mum and dad, for all those *Doctor Who* books, and for the phone booth made of asbestos you bought for me to play in.

Thank you to my children, Redvers and Ash, for teaching me what it's like to create life and then be unable to control it. Thank you to Venetia, my lab assistant in this ongoing experiment. (Okay, okay. *You're* the mad scientist; *I'm* the assistant.)

Thank you to the ingenious Clare Forster, who somehow knew I could write this book, and to the indefatigable Talia Moodley and Alexandra Christie, who saw the project through. Much love to the extraordinary team at Curtis Brown (Australia). Shovels all round!

Thank you to the endlessly enthusiastic Tom Rawlinson and the eagle-eyed and creative Beth Axford, as well as Philippa Neville, Vicki Vrint, Lucy Doncaster, Debs Warner and all the wonderful people at Penguin Random House UK. It's an honour to be trusted with these characters. I may have stitched this book together, but you electrified it.

Acknowledgements

Thank you to the irrepressible George Ivanoff for sharing his time and his unparalleled knowledge of Trakenite linguistic anomalies, and to my brother Tom, whose understanding of the Doctor puts my own to shame.

About the Author

Jack Heath is the award-winning author of more than forty books, which have been translated into ten languages. He lives on Ngunnawal/Ngambri land in Australia with his wife, five chickens, three possums, two cats and a pair of human children.

Find him at jackheathwriter.com and @jackheathwriter on social media.

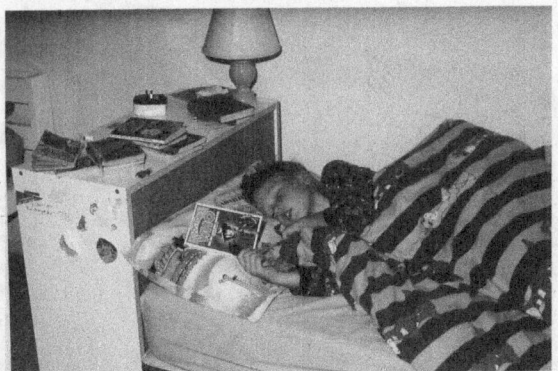

Photo of Jack as a boy with his *Doctor Who* books, taken by Barbara Davidson, 1995

Turn the page for an extract from another classics story and *Doctor Who* crossover ...

An unknown cosmic foe has trapped the Doctor and his companions in a twisted version of Alice's Wonderland.

Separated from the TARDIS and from each other, their only hope of escape lies in cryptic clues teased by fan-favourite characters from Carroll's classic tale.

Chapter One

The boy had been trapped on planet Earth for so long that he'd almost forgotten what it was like to voyage across outer space.

He had been eleven years old when he was first dropped off in London by his people. There, he came under the care of a strange, elderly solicitor. Shortly after that, he was dumped at some supposedly fancy boarding school in the countryside, which turned out to be full of dull, idiotic people he had quickly come to despise. Why were Earth people so boring? It was all filling out forms, doing exams and playing pointless games with them. As he grew up and became a teenager, Turlough began to lose hope of ever having any fun ever again.

By the time he was studying for his A levels, he was at his wits' end. By then, he had become a skinny, acid-tongued, furious youth. He longed to rebel and cause some trouble — but how, exactly? And what was the point? He could run rings around his schoolmasters, who were a plodding, ancient lot. They all carried on as if they belonged to the Victorian era with their mortar boards and tweedy suits. This was the

1980s! Turlough had made several attempts to return to London and into the fun he imagined must be happening there, but they always dragged him back again.

Then came the day that he and his hopeless friend Hippo stole the maths teacher's prized sports car and managed to escape. It gave them a brief, exciting moment of freedom! Whizzing down the country lanes at top speed, he had laughed — actually laughed! — for the first time in months, because he had managed to get beyond those vast, imposing school gates.

But then the stupid vehicle malfunctioned and he'd ended up in a ditch. The car was a write-off. It was just as well, because it had been a rubbish old thing anyway, really. However, the most important thing about the car crash was that, aside from receiving a mild concussion, Turlough had found himself in a bewilderingly strange dimension for a few moments, looking down upon the scene of the accident. There was everyone down below, fussing over the crumpled car and foolish, unharmed Hippo — and here was Turlough, hovering above them all.

Am I dead? he wondered silently, just as he became aware of a dark and terrible presence looming over him. It was hovering right beside him. He hardly dared look at the being who had come to haunt him. A claw-like hand was upon his shoulder and a dreadful voice was suddenly rumbling in his ear.

It was a voice that spoke to him cajolingly, telling him impossible things. A voice that belonged to a being who persuaded Turlough to make a terrible bargain. Turlough was left with nothing but a small white, glowing crystal. It was the only proof he needed that his dark visitor was real. It was a reminder of the promise he had made.

Shivering, Turlough shook himself out of his awful reverie. No, it was no use dwelling on all of that. It was an entire week later and everything was different now. His whole life had changed, more than it had in years, and ultimately he was glad.

Now he was a traveller aboard the TARDIS. He was a crew member aboard a mysterious kind of time machine. It was an amazingly advanced craft that was much larger on the inside than the outside. This was unbelievably exciting, and he was doing everything he could to contain his glee and maintain an aloof and slightly superior attitude. But he had actually escaped! He had made a bargain and come through several awful ordeals and now here he was aboard this amazing vessel. All of time and space were his to explore!

There were, of course, a number of drawbacks and irritations, as there often were in his life.

First of all – and he didn't want to dwell on it – there was the constant threat from the being whom he had first encountered in that weird dimension after the slight accident in the maths teacher's car. But he wasn't thinking about that just now. No, he could put all of that out of his mind. He was even trying to convince himself that it had all been just a bizarre dream.

The other complications in his immediate future had to do with his three travelling companions aboard the TARDIS.

As he wandered the seemingly endless corridors of the time ship, he made a list of them in his head. The TARDIS crew consisted of:

1. Nyssa, who was sweet and trusting. It almost embarrassed Turlough how easy she'd been to hoodwink into thinking he was just an innocent schoolboy with no ulterior motives or evil plans at all. She came from Traken or somewhere soppy like that, where everyone believed in peace and harmony. Naturally, the whole place had been blown up during some previous adventure and Nyssa was a homeless orphan, very much like Turlough. He supposed he found her endearing in a way.
2. Tegan, who was brash, argumentative and Australian. Turlough knew for a fact that she didn't trust him an inch. She looked at him as if her eyes were drilling into him, like she was still trying to work him out. 'I know you're up to something,' she had hissed at him several times when she thought no one else was about. He would have to work harder on winning her over.
3. Lastly, of course, there was the Doctor. He was younger than Turlough had expected. From what he'd been told, he had expected someone older and more wicked-looking. Someone easier to dislike. But the person in command of this ramshackle time-space vessel was a pleasant, affable young man who wore cricketing whites and had a stick of celery pinned to the lapel of his coat. He was sincere, brimming with enthusiasm and quite impossible to hate. Now that he had gotten to

In Wonderland

know the Time Lord a little, it was going to be extremely hard for Turlough to carry out his secret mission. But he knew he simply had to do as he was commanded. He had to find the right moment in which to murder the Doctor.

Turlough sighed heavily and paused in his exploration of the glowing labyrinth. What day was it? Tuesday? He'd always hated Tuesdays. They seemed more complicated and annoying than every other day of the week.

He opened an exceptionally plain white door, seemingly the same as every other door he had encountered on his explorations. But beyond this one lay the wonders of the TARDIS library.

Nyssa had announced hours ago that she was off to the library. She wanted to spend a few hours relaxing, away from the rigours of TARDIS travel. She desired to read something about bio-electronics or some such. Turlough hadn't heard the exact details, but it sounded quite serious and complicated. He was pretty clever himself, and he had spent the past eight years trying to cover up the fact that he knew more about science than his schoolmasters ever would. In the case of Nyssa and the Doctor though, he knew he was in the presence of seriously clever people. Tegan was dopey, but she was shrewd.

'You're going to relax by reading about science?' Tegan had laughed her braying laugh at Nyssa. 'Why don't you read something fun?'

Nyssa frowned as if the concept was alien to her. 'Fun?'

The Doctor was looking concerned. 'Yes, you must make sure you relax, Nyssa. We've been through some rather testing escapades just lately. You have to be careful not to over-tax the old grey matter, you know.'

Nyssa shrugged. 'What would you suggest?'

'I know . . .!' Tegan had dashed off to fetch a beautiful first edition of a novel she had recently found in a cluttered, dusty corner of the TARDIS. 'I read this when I was a kid. I just loved it. It's an Earth classic! You've got to read it!'

Nyssa took the ancient hardback book, pulling a puzzled face. 'Isn't this a children's book . . .?'

The Doctor beamed at her. 'As a very wise man once said to me, "What's the point in being grown-up if you can't be childish sometimes?", hmm?' He took the book carefully and turned to an inscription on the fly-life. 'Goodness, this is a first edition. Belonged to Victoria, I see.' He handed it back to Nyssa. 'Reading this will do you more good than any amount of bio-engineering abstracts.'

'I wonder if I can find it in a data cube edition . . .' Nyssa had pondered, and wandered off in the direction of the library. And now, several hours later, Turlough had discovered her, fast asleep on a comfortable sofa in the deepest corner of the room.

The TARDIS library was a magnificent place. It made Turlough hold his breath like he was in some amazing, sacred kind of space. Bookcases rose several storeys high towards a ceiling obscured by curling mist. There were tables and cosy chairs and golden-glowing lamps. Random heaps of books and periodicals of all kinds littered the place. Not just books, either – there were discs and cubes and all manner of futuristic devices designed to deliver text and information directly into the reader's mind.

When Turlough crept closer to the sleeping Trakenite he realised that she had tried to read the book suggested by Tegan in several different formats. The hardback book was lying splayed open on the couch beside her. It did look like a very valuable volume indeed. Gingerly, Turlough picked it up.

'Alice's Adventures in Wonderland,' he read aloud. 'By Lewis Carroll.' Well, naturally he was aware of it. He'd never read it, of course. It looked like silly nonsense, kids' stuff. He had avoided all the reading suggestions he had ever been given, just as he had refused to do most of the homework he had ever been set. The very thought of Tegan saying she had enjoyed reading this book was enough to set his teeth on edge. It must be a rotten old book to evoke happy memories in someone like her.

Still, Turlough felt compelled to flick through the pages of the vintage tome. It had elaborate line drawings, rather silly ones. There were birds, beasts and all kinds of weird, impossible things. No wonder it had made Nyssa nod off. It was probably giving her nightmares. He glanced down at the sleeping girl, but she seemed gently serene.

Turlough envied her. He hadn't had a good night's sleep in ages and – what with the way things were – he doubted he would rest well again any time soon.

Just then, as if on cue, he felt a heavy hand upon his shoulder. He almost dropped the heavy book in fright. A very deep, sepulchral voice boomed inside his head: 'I am still here, boy. I haven't forgotten you. I hope you haven't forgotten the promise you made to me.'

Turlough found himself whining and squirming. 'Leave me alone . . . *please* . . .!'

'*Never!*' roared the entity who had pursued him like a shadow. 'You're not getting away from me, boy. It's time to get to work on the next phase of my plan.' He snarled. 'That decayed volume of ancient wisdom you are clutching in your feeble grasp has given me a rather good idea . . .' The Black Guardian threw his head back and began to laugh demonically while the runaway schoolboy cringed in fear.

Chapter Two

The main control room of the TARDIS was a large, gleaming white space dominated by a multi-sided console. A column made of glass filled with sophisticated instrumentation rose and fell whenever the ship was in flight. It was doing so right now, quite serenely, as the crew went about their business, and the TARDIS tumbled through the vortex, that mysterious region where time and space were one.

To Turlough, the whole place looked like it could do with a bit of refurbishment. There were scorch marks and obvious damage recently caused by something called 'the Cybermen'. Several buttons were missing and various dials and levers had broken off or got stuck when you tried to budge them. He studied the control panels carefully, trying to make sense of them all. In his hand, he was holding the white crystal he had received a week ago. When he held it in his palm, he could communicate directly with his master. The chunk of crystal glowed hotly, that awful voice reverberating inside his head: 'Take out the book in its liquid form.'

Nyssa had found various editions of *Alice's Adventures in Wonderland* – paper, electronic and otherwise. Among them had been an intriguing little bottle. It was dark pink and labelled 'Drink Me'. Turlough had pocketed it under instruction, but it was the kind of thing that would have caught his eye and ended up in his possession anyway. 'How can a book come in the form of a solution?' he asked the presence inside his mind.

'This might prove to be the solution to both our problems,' the ominous presence chuckled with a rare flash of dark humour.

Turlough removed the small stopper and sniffed the contents of the container. The stuff inside smelled like raspberry jam and custard! Jelly and cream cakes! Lemonade and sunshine! His hand trembled and he dropped it on to the console.

'*Foolish* boy,' laughed the being from within.

The dark rosy liquid had splashed on to the control panels and was fizzing as it evaporated. It seemed to be sinking into the shining metal of the console. The bottle had shattered on contact and its shards were scattered everywhere. Turlough swore and hissed at the white crystal: 'You *made* me do that! You made me drop it . . .'

The creature in his head guffawed at the very suggestion. He was fading away now, as he often did when he decided that their conversation was at an end.

Turlough stared at the console, watching the last of the pink liquid somehow soak into the metal, and with a wisp of mist, it simply faded away. The time rotor made a decisive noise – almost a sigh of satisfaction – and began to descend. The TARDIS was shifting gear, slowing down. It was preparing to emerge from the vortex into normal space-time, Turlough realised.

In Wonderland

The interior door flew open and the Doctor strode into the room. 'We're about to land!' he beamed at his newest companion. *He was so trusting*, Turlough thought to himself. *Was he really that foolish?* Turlough felt shifty standing there alone at the console. Even *he* realised that he looked as if he was up to something.

'Soon be there!' the Doctor cried, examining various illuminated panels. '*Hmmm.*'

Then came the distinctive wheezing, groaning noise that Turlough recognised as the ship coming in to land. 'Where are we?' he asked the Time Lord.

'I won't know that until we've fully materialised,' the Doctor replied.

'You don't even know . . .?' Turlough tried his best to keep the scorn out of his voice.

'Well, that's half the adventure . . .' the Doctor enthused. At this point, Nyssa and Tegan both arrived in the console room. Nyssa looked refreshed after her nap in the library, and Tegan looked cross as a result of whatever she had been getting up to. 'Explain to Turlough,' the Doctor said. 'Tell him how much fun it is, never really knowing where we might end up.'

'Oh, it's a hoot,' Tegan rolled her eyes.

'It can be quite invigorating!' Nyssa smiled. 'What's that strange smell . . .?' She sniffed the air. There was still a trace of the gloopy fluid that Turlough had spilt. 'It reminds me of . . .' She drifted away, trying to catch the tail end of a memory.

'Hey, how was the book?' Tegan asked her friend. 'Could you get into it?'

Nyssa feigned enthusiasm. 'Well, I found it quite confusing, to be honest. It was so illogical and strange. I couldn't see why half the things were even happening . . .'

Tegan laughed at her perplexity. 'That's how it's meant to be. It's not supposed to make sense. I remember reading it when I was a kid, in the middle of nowhere on my father's sheep farm. Books like *Alice* – especially *Alice* – were where I could escape to . . . away from all the monotony . . .'

The Doctor was bustling around the console. He produced his Panama hat and jammed it on to his long blond hair. 'Enough time for reminiscences about the outback later!' He laughed. 'Right now, we've got somewhere new to explore.'

Turlough straightened his tie and buttoned up his blazer. 'And where *is* that exactly . . .?'

Peering at the instruments, the Doctor was surprised to find some brittle shards of broken glass. Much of the bottle Turlough had smashed had vanished into the air, but these few pieces remained. They were sticky to the touch. 'Hullo, what's this?' asked the Doctor. He took out a large spotted handkerchief and gathered the pieces up. All this mess was a bit close to the ultra-sensitive psychic circuits for his liking. Why did his companions have to be so messy?

'According to the TARDIS, we're on Earth in the nineteenth century,' Nyssa told them all.

Tegan's expression went dark. Nothing she'd seen in her previous visit to the nineteenth century made her want to return to it.

'Earth?' Turlough sneered. He had been longing to see other worlds again and to put as much distance as possible

In Wonderland

between himself and this poky backwater planet that thought so much of itself.

The Doctor absent-mindedly popped the hanky full of glass shards into his coat pocket and stared at the instruments. 'Oh! Now, this is something of an amazing coincidence. You know, it's really quite remarkable. If I didn't know better, I'd swear that the old girl had been listening in on our recent conversations.'

Turlough was puzzled. 'What "old girl"?'

Tegan laughed. 'It's what the Doctor calls the TARDIS. He behaves like she's a real person. I thought he was crazy at first . . .'

The Doctor glared at her. 'But now you know better, hmm?' He activated the door control with a tender pat.

Tegan laughed and followed the Doctor, who was leading the others out through the TARDIS doors.

They emerged into brilliant autumn sunshine, which made them blink and smile. Trees rustled overhead and the battered blue police box shell of the TARDIS had materialised beside the entrance of a park. They faced out on to a bustling street, where horses and carriages and people in stiff Victorian clothes were all too busy or much too well-mannered to notice the arrival of a mysterious time machine.

Turlough was still getting used to the oddity of travelling inside something no larger than a confessional box or a phone booth. 'It's so . . . incongruous,' he muttered.

'That's why we like it.' The Doctor smiled at him, locking the doors securely.

Tegan was studying the spires and rooftops around them. They seemed ancient and well-preserved to her. 'Are we in London?' she asked.

'Oxford,' the Doctor told her. 'That's why I said it's as if the TARDIS had been listening to our conversation. This is Oxford, 1862. And that, if I'm not very much mistaken, is the entrance to Christ Church college.'

Nyssa joined them to study the buildings. 'Isn't this where I was just reading about?'

'More or less,' the Doctor told her. 'It's where that story all began, at any rate.'

'But isn't that a bit weird?' Tegan said. 'I mean, if you're right about the TARDIS listening . . . that creeps me out a little bit.'

The Doctor looked hurt. 'Creeps you out?' He dashed back to stroke the side of his police box. 'Never mind, old girl. Don't listen to her.'

Turlough stared at his companions with disbelief. They were all enjoying their banter enormously. To him it seemed very silly and a waste of precious time. 'What are we going to do here?' he asked.

'Do?' The Doctor smiled. 'Why, we shall explore! Let's take a stroll, shall we?'

He turned first one way, and then the next, as if testing the air with an expert nose for the ideal route to take. Deciding upon the best direction, he set off briskly up a cobbled lane between narrow houses. Turlough hurried after him, wondering if the two women were dressed altogether appropriately for this historical era.

In Wonderland

'Stop dallying behind, Turlough!' called the Doctor, as if he was leading a tour party. 'You know, I haven't been here since the nineteen fifties,' the Time Lord mused. 'I wonder if it's changed much?'

They mooched about for much of that morning, peering into the windows of interesting-looking buildings and rummaging in bookshops. They paused on a bridge and looked down into the bronze waters and drifting green weed. Nyssa was staring at the passing boats. 'Oh! I'd love to do that. What do you call that?'

'Boating?' Turlough laughed. 'Punting? Are you saying you've never seen anyone punting before?'

She shook her head. Nyssa was sometimes self-conscious about her limited experiences growing up on Traken. Some of the things her companions in the TARDIS took for granted were entirely novel to her.

'Well!' the Doctor said. 'Before we leave here we must see that you take a trip up the river, Nyssa. You'll love it, I'm sure. How do you feel about punting, Turlough?'

'He doesn't look the type to me,' Tegan said snippily.

'I'll have you know I'm sure I'd be rather good at it!' he replied hotly. 'I've got marvellous coordination.'

Tegan rolled her eyes and led the way to a little shop she had spotted across the road. She peeped through the mullioned windows at rows of baked treats of all kinds. 'I've just realised I'm starving.'

Inside, they found a small room with shelves closely packed with boxes and jars. There was a delicious smell of baking that drifted in from a kitchen behind the main counter. An old woman was sitting hunched at the huge till, wrapped in a woolly shawl and peering at the newcomers over her old-fashioned spectacles. 'We're all sold out,' she snapped at them. Her teeth were long and yellow, rather like the sheep Tegan remembered from her father's farm.

'Sold out of what?' Tegan asked. 'Your shop window's chockablock with cakes! We only want a few . . .'

'Sold out! All gone!' the old shopkeeper cried. In fact, the closer Tegan stared through the gloom of the little shop, the more the old woman looked exactly like a sheep. A peevish old ewe who didn't want to sell them any delicious cakes.

'You've got loads!' Tegan retorted.

'Tegan,' the Doctor warned her. 'If the nice lady says she's sold out, then . . .'

'What kind of a way to run a business is that?' Tegan tutted.

'All the cakes are waiting to be taken away,' the shopkeeper told them. 'My entire stock of cream buns and jam tarts. They're all spoken for.'

'Ah, I see,' said the Doctor.

'There's a big tea party,' the sheepish old woman went on. 'Over at the deanery. The Dean of Christ Church. The one with all the pretty daughters. They're having a fancy do. They want all the cakes! All my cakes are off to be eaten at the party, so I'm sorry for you, but I can't spare a single one!'

'Well, never mind,' said Tegan, who had heard quite enough from the old woman by now.

The Doctor was staring at the shopkeeper with a strange look painted across his face. 'The Dean of Christ Church is throwing a grand tea party, is he?'

'This afternoon,' the old woman replied. 'Don't you have an invitation? All the great, the good and the very clever will be there this afternoon. Oh yes, indeed. They'll all be there, whooping it up!'

'Why yes,' said the Doctor with a delighted smile. 'I do believe we *are* invited, yes! So maybe we'll get to try your appetising cakes after all.'

The shopkeeper bared her dreadful teeth at him. 'Then perhaps, if you're going there, you could help me out? You could do me a favour?'

Tegan was about to refuse outright, but the Doctor was in his most charming mode. 'What would you like us to do?'

'My usual delivery boy has let me down today. I've seen neither hide nor hair of him all morning. Perhaps you and your young friends could take these trays over to Christ Church deanery for me? Would you mind delivering the cakes?'

The Doctor smiled broadly. 'We would be delighted!'

The shopkeeper let out a bleat of relief. 'Oh good! But time is running on, you know. Oh, look at the time! You'd best hurry up! All of you young people! Take these cakes, at once! Hurry! Otherwise, you'll be late! You'll be much too late for the party!'

'What's so important about the cakes being on time?' Nyssa asked.

The old woman responded: 'There is talk that Her Majesty herself will be in attendance . . .!'

DISCOVER THE REST OF THE PUFFIN CLASSICS AND *DOCTOR WHO* CROSSOVER RANGE

DOCTOR WHO

Dracula!

By Paul Magrs

COMING AUGUST 2025